A SLICE OF LIFE

An Anthology of Short Stories

Edited by

DR. RADHA MOHAN SINGH

Professor and Head Department of English

Patna University, Patna

DR. SATYA BRAT SINGH

Professor and Head Department of English

Tilka Manjhi University, Bhagalpur

DR. MUNIBA SAMI

Reader in English

Patna University

MOTILAL BANARSIDASS

Delhi • Mumbai • Chennai • Kolkata

Bengaluru • Varanasi • Patna

3rd Reprint: Delhi, 2017
First Edition: 2010

ISBN: 978-81-208-3471-2

MOTILAL BANARSIDASS
41 U.A., Bungalow Road, Jawahar Nagar, Delhi 110 007
8 Mahalaxmi Chamber, 22 Bhulabhai Desai Road, Mumbai 400 026
203 Royapettah High Road, Mylapore, Chennai 600 004
236, 9th Main III Block, Jayanagar, Bengaluru 560 011
8 Camac Street, Kolkata 700 017
Ashok Rajpath, Patna 800 004
Chowk, Varanasi 221 001

Printed in India
by RP Jain at NAB Printing Unit,
A-44, Naraina Industrial Area, Phase I, New Delhi–110028
and published by JP Jain for Motilal Banarsidass
41 U.A. Bungalow Road, Jawahar Nagar, Delhi-110007

PREFACE

The present anthology of stories has been prepared for students at the tertiary and undergraduate levels. The anthology introduces to the reader some of the best short stories written by famous authors of recent times. These stories are representative of the fine art of story writing and the different techniques adopted by the masters of story-telling. They bring out the morals and values that are held in high esteem by all.

The stories have been especially designed to suit the needs of students for whom English is a second language. Brief biographies of the authors, a comprehensive glossary have been added as study aids. We are confident that teachers will enjoy teaching the fascinating stories here and students will enjoy and appreciate the works of our best writers.

We will consider our efforts amply rewarded if the present work conveys the message embedded in these priceless reflections of the human mind.

—Authors

CONTENTS

□

INTRODUCTION

The Indian short story in English, though a late-comer on the literary scene, exhibits an astonishing range of subject matter and wide variety of techniques. Though often considered a derivative of its western counterpart, it is not a hot-house plant but manifests a striking resemblance in its genius to the story written in any Indian language. No wonder, our literary historians trace its genesis to ancient Indian classics like the Panchatantra, the fables of Brihatkatha, Kathasaritsagar or Yoga-Vashistha. These ancient stories for the most part conform in their structure to the Aristotelian prescription-an incisive beginning, middle and end-with their story-line suggestive of a palpable moral. Their plots are not elliptical or metaphoric, as defined by critics like Suzanne Ferguson. Their primary impulsion is didactic; their Endeavour is to instruct rather than entertain.

The short story, written in the Indian languages, acquiring the form of a distinct literary genre, however, emerged only in the quarter of the nineteenth century. It was mostly influenced by Western writers, British or American. If, for instance, Bankimchandra Chatterjee could be said to have been influenced by Sir Walter Scott, Rabindranath Tagore could be found susceptible to the influence of his won favorite British writers. In fact, before the end of the century, most short fiction written in the Indian languages, particularly in Hindi, Urdu, Bengali or Tamil, carried the impress of such masters as Chekhov, Tolstoy, Maupassant, O'Henry and Kipling. It is not surprising, therefore, that the early short story, written in English or any Indian language, kept close to the formulistic in design, hardly ever delving deep into the character's psyche. The entire structure was patently conditioned by the author's own penchant-moral, religious, sociological or political. Consequently, it groaned under such constraints as would not allow the characters to breathe freely. Further, the author's concern with consistency kept his characters always on the leash, and within the restrictive range of the story-line. The result was that the story read more like an 'argument' than an 'impression' to use Thomas Hardy's terms to emphasize the impressionistic freedom of a genuine work of art which, incidentally, his own work lacked.

So the early short story, whether written in English or any Indian language, grew under Western tutelage. The only difference was that while the writer in the Indian language breathed in the

Western influence as a part of the Zeitgeist, the writer in English was ostensibly conscious of his indebtedness to the Western masters. "There was the impact on me of Maupassant. Frank O'Connor and Theodore Powys," observes Mulk Raj Anand, one of the pioneers of this art. Similarly, one may trace the influence of Chekhov on R.K. Narayan, or of the French masters or Raja Rao. But one must hasten to add that although this distinguished triumvirate-Anand, Narayan and Rao-had used a foreign medium for creative expression, and often displayed Western technical virtuosity in their craft, their innate genius never felt smothered. If Tagore wrote as a folk storyteller, never refracting the psychology of his characters to suit a Western audience, Mulk Raj Anand remained firmly committed to social reality, investing his coolies and untouchables with a vibrant humanity that he found lacking in the upper classes. As for Raja Rao, he shaped the English language to suit the Indian sensibility, investing it with a fluidity and suppleness that was foreign to it. In his Foreword to Kanthapura, he brilliantly expounds his concept of what might be called Indian-English, and the Indian 'tempo'.

A cursory glance at the state of affairs obtaining in Indian English short story convinces the reader that it has traversed a long course of journey (nearly of one hundred years) and has now reached a stage through the salutary efforts of a few talented writers, where it can make a breakthrough by exploring certain new areas and techniques. Despite the natural hardships of language and expression - remember, English is your acquired tongue, not mother tongue as such - the short story has made some headway and has become truly Indian after shaking off the initial foreign influences. The short story writers have come to realize, and rightly so, that their own tradition of both folk-tales and fables has been rich enough to feed and support them in moments of necessity, and that they have just to look around for their keen and lively subjects, to which they have tailored their modern techniques. So, while their sensibility and subject-matter are essentially 'autochthonous', their treatment of stories is moulded by such modern modes of expression as the stream-of-consciousness, the flashback and flashforth, the first person narration, the point-of-view method, and the epistolary method. The traditional Indian tale used to be mostly didactic and descriptive in nature, but the modern story tends to be analytical and narrative. As against the omniscient author technique of a traditional tale, we find a number of other techniques in our day. This shows that the modern Indian short story in English has grown in variety and vitality, and credit for this mainly goes to the 'Big Three' and Isvaran and a few other gifted writers. But it would be a misconception if we think that this form has reached the pinnacle of artistic perfection and that nothing more is required to be done in it. Most of the writers have confined themselves to social scenes and events; they have ignored certain other burning issues of the day, such as the political awakening and upheavals during the pre-Independence and post-Independence periods. Also, they have largely overlooked 'the purely domestic situation', but for Anand's "Lajwanti" and Raja Rao's "Akkayya" and Jhabvala's "The Interview". In their desire to be indigenous, these writers have occasionally grown over-enthusiastic and sentimental; in their inherent urge to be impressive, they have resorted to word-jugglery and verbosity. Many writers have felt the constraints of 'journalism' because they have to be readable to general public through the medium of magazines and periodicals. While such a tendency contributes lucidity and clarity to their writings, they come to suffer on counts of complexity, subtlety and suggestiveness, - a point which becomes crystal-clear to an alert reader making a comparative study of an Indian author with his counterpart in the West. Our writers have unquestionably added variety of theme and diversity of technique to this art-form, but they have yet to rise above some of the shortcomings listed above. They have yet to cultivate the qualities of brevity, economy and signification in their works in order to be able to compete with the international masters of the genre - Maupassant, Faulkner, Henry James, Hemingway, Galsworthy and Katherine Mansfield.

Finally, contemporary Indian short story in English is already standing at the crossroads, and it has to make cautious moves to pull itself through. Keeping in view the international standards, it has to strive consistently to arrive at a safe destination. For this, it will have to overcome its deficiencies and evolve fresh measures of invigoration and energisation. We have only to 'wait and watch' for a better future of the short story, and not get bogged down in the morasses of unhealthy speculations and pessimistic tendencies, realizing the truth that 'The best is yet to come'.

'What Is a Short Story?'

The literary form short story is usually defined as a brief fictional prose narrative, often involving one connected episode. Early in the nineteenth century the American writer Edgar Allan Poe was one of the first to attempt an analysis of the short story's aesthetic properties. He stressed unity of effect as the story's most characteristic feature. Since the flood of events we experience in life is rarely unified by a single impression, in a sense all fiction - whether short story, long story, or novel - is "lies." Paradoxically, however, the measure of success for all fiction is how true it is to our emotions, how accurately it reflects the life that is lived by all of us.

The short story is a concentrated form, dependent for its success on feeling and suggestion. When readers are responsive to both the story and its writer and understand the ways an author uses language to create a fictional world, the unity of the story has an even greater impact. Then every detail of the narrative adds to our enjoyment of the story's final impression. Writers of short stories must forgo the comprehensiveness of the novel, but they often gain a striking compression by using language with the force of poetry. Like poets, short story writers can impress upon us the unity of their vision of life by focusing on a single effect.

Although storytelling is one of the oldest arts, not every story or short narrative is necessarily an example of what has come to be known as the short story. The modern short story is comparatively new in literature, even younger than the novel. It originated in the early years of the nineteenth centenary, and its vitality may have sprung from the spirit of its age, which nurtured the Romantic movement in literature and valued imagination above all other qualities in writing.

This anthology begins with stories form the period when professional writers began experimenting with forms of short fictional narrative in both Europe and America. Nathaniel Hawthorne and Edgar Allan Poe were among the earliest American authors to achieve success in the genre. In the nineteenth and twentieth centuries, most of the great writers of fiction throughout the world explored the short story. This anthology is organized chronologically to suggest the historical evolution of the form, presenting examples by some of its most notable practitioners. The head notes for the authors suggest their personal and intellectual backgrounds and their intentions as writers of short fiction.

Fifty years after its earliest appearance, the short story reached maturity in the work of Guy de Maupassant and Anton Chekhov. It flowered into perhaps its most intense expression in the stories of the great modernist writers of the early twentieth century - James Joyce, Franz Kafka, D. H. Lawrence, Katherine Mansfield, Isaac Babel, and Ernest Hemingway, to name only a few of the great innovators who experimented with the structure and texture of literature and challenged its conventions. The short story continues to flourish in the work of many gifted contemporary writers, attracting more attention than ever before.

The range and quality of the writer's mind are the only limitations on the shape taken by a story. In the process of creation, authors invent narratives using the different elements of fiction. Among their most important resources are plot, the sequence of related events composing the narrative, and characters, the persons who play their parts in the narrative. The author's choice of setting, the place and time in which the story's action occurs, helps to give the story verisimilitude. The point of view establishes a consistent perspective on the characters and their actions as the narrative unfolds. The author's literary style, the way he or she uses the multifarious resources of language, also shapes the expression of a story. Finally, the author is guided by his or her perception of theme, the unifying idea that brings to life all the other elements of fiction.

Without human understanding, experience is "the worst kind of emptiness," wrote the short story author Eudora Welty in her essay "Words into Fiction." All stories embody a personal vision, when the elements of plot, character, setting, point of view, style, and theme are set in motion by the writer's perception of the mystery and magic of everyday life. Creating fiction, authors are free to invent and shape experience to the fullest extent of their imagination. The section of commentaries following the stories in the anthology includes many statements by writers about the meaning and form of their fiction.

Human understanding is not the exclusive privilege of the writer, of course. It functions in the reader too. Fiction created by the imagination of the writer for the imagination of the reader is an illusion that comes full circle. If the story is well told, our imagination will be involved. If the story is a success, our imagination will be ignited.

The Short Story has assumed the importance of a literary symbol of the modern time. Social conditions of modern age and individualistic tendency of the modern man have proved very congenial to its development. Busy life of the industrial age, life spent in bits and moments, additional importance attached to the otherwise ordinary incidents of life, short span of leisure at our disposal, impatience of the modern man, preference for shorter forms etc. are some of the factors which have given a tremendous push to this form of fiction. Moreover, short story has certain advantages over other forms of literature. No form of literature has more immediate appeal than the short story. A poem may be more deeply suggestive, but it calls for careful reading and re-reading to be fully apprehended. A novel may sustain a reader's interest for hours or days, but its total effect is massive and general rather than sharp and direct. In the short story the reader can experience a situation both briefly and intensely. A poem insinuates, a novel pushes, but a short story hits. To read and enjoy a short story requires neither the effort that poetry demands nor the time that is required by a novel.

Besides, the short story has a variety, which certain other forms lack. It has the potentiality of satisfying multifarious tastes of the readers. So much so that certain critics apprehend the danger of its replacing novel. But it seems to be a big hope, which the modern short story may not and should not fulfill, as the scope of the two-short story and novel-is entirely different.

A short story is neither a summary nor a part of a novel. It has a separate and independent entity. It may be defined as that modern and dramatic form of fiction in which the incidents are arranged in such a way that with its one dominant incident or character it is able to achieve brevity. With singleness of purpose and oneness of impression. It presents a slice of life, which has beauty and truth-qualities stressed by Keats as, "All that we know on earth and all that we need to know."

That way, the short story has a splendid vogue in modern times. It is growing more and more popular both with the readers and writers. It caters to all interests psychological, sociological and scientific, humanitarian, regional and exotic. It is specially suited to modern life. For minds that have little time and less inclination for spacious indulgences, the concentrated form of the short story in a boon. Literary history is a warning against prophecies, but it can be safely asserted that the short story has an immensely rich future. Its variety and vividness shall continue to grant to it a recognized place and position.

□

1. THE DIAMOND NECKLACE

(Guy De Maupassant)

She was one of those pretty and charming girls who, by some freak of destiny, are born into families that have always held subordinate appointments. Possessing neither dowry nor expectations, she had no hope of meeting some man of wealth and distinction, who would understand her, fall in love with her, and wed her. So she consented to marry a small clerk in the Ministry of Public Instruction.

She dressed plainly, because she could not afford to be elegant, but she felt as unhappy as if she had married beneath her. Women are dependent neither on caste nor ancestry. With them, beauty, grace and charm take the place of birth and breeding. In their case, natural delicacy, instinctive refinement and adaptability constitute their claims to aristocracy and raise girls of the lower classes to an equality with the greatest of great ladies. She was eternally restive under the conviction that she had been born to enjoy every refinement and luxury. Depressed by her humble surroundings, the sordid walls of her dwelling, its worn furniture and shabby hangings were a torment to her. Details which another woman of her class would scarcely have noticed, tortured her and filled her with resentment. The sight of her little Breton maid-of-all-work roused in her forlorn repinings and frantic yearnings. She pictured to herself silent antechambers, upholstered with oriental tapestry, lighted by great bronze standard lamps, while two tall footmen in knee-breeches slumbered in huge arm-chairs, overcome by the oppressive heat from the stove. She dreamed of spacious drawing-rooms with hangings of antique silk, and beautiful tables laden with priceless ornaments; of fragrant and coquettish boudoirs, exquisitely adapted for afternoon chats with intimate friends, men of note and distinction, whose attentions are coveted by every woman.

She would sit down to dinner at the round table, its cloth already three days old, while her husband, seated opposite to her, removed the lid from the soup tureen and exclaimed, "How splendid! My favourite soup!" But her own thoughts were dallying with the idea of exquisite dinners and shining silver, in rooms whose tapestried walls were gay with antique figures and grotesque birds in fairy forests. She would dream of delicious dishes served on wonderful plate, of soft, whispered nothings, which evoke a sphinx-like smile, while one trifles with the pink flesh of a trout or the wing of a plump pullet.

She had no pretty gowns, no jewels, nothing—and yet she cared for nothing else. She felt that it was for such things as these that she had been born. What joy it would have given her to attract, to charm, to be envied by women, courted by men! She had a wealthy friend, who had been at school at the same convent, but after a time she refused to go and see her, because she suffered so acutely after each visit. She spent whole days in tears of grief, regret, despair and misery.

One evening her husband returned home in triumph with a large envelope in his hand.

"Here is something for you." he cried.

Hastily she tore open the envelope and drew out a printed card with the following inscription:

"The Minister of Public Instruction and Madame George Ramponneau have the honour to request the company of Monsieur and Madam Loisel at an At Home at the Education Office on Monday, January 18th."

Instead of being delighted, as her husband had hoped, she flung the invitation irritably on the table, exclaiming:

"What good is that to me?"

"Why, my dear, I thought you would be pleased. You never go anywhere, and this is a really splendid chance for you. I had no end of trouble in getting it. Everybody is trying to get an invitation. It's very select, and only a few invitations are issued to the clerks. You will see all the officials there."

She looked at him in exasperation, and exclaimed petulantly:

"What do you expect me to wear at a reception like that?"

He had not considered the matter, but he replied hesitatingly:

"Why, that dress you always wear to the theatre seems to me very nice indeed ......"

He broke off. To his horror and consternation he saw that his wife was in tears. Two large drops were rolling slowly down her cheeks.

"What on earth is the matter?" he gasped.

With a violent effort she controlled her emotion, and drying her wet cheeks said in a calm voice:

"Nothing. Only I haven't a frock, and so I can't go to the reception. Give your invitation to some friend in your office whose wife is better dressed than I am."

He was greatly distressed.

"Let us talk it over, Mitilda. How much do you think a proper frock would cost, something quite simple that might come in useful for other occasions afterwards?"

She considered the matter for a few moments, busy with her calculations, and wondering how large a sum she might venture to name without shocking the little clerk's instincts of economy and provoking a prompt refusal.

"I hardly know." she said at last doubtfully, "but I think I could manage with four hundred francs."

He turned a little pale, She had named the exact sum that he had saved for buying a gun and making up Sunday shooting parties the following summer with some friends who were going to shoot larks in the plain of Nanterre.

But he replied :

"Very well, I'll give you four hundred francs. But mind you buy a really handsome gown."

* * * * *

The day of the party drew near. But although her gown was finished, Madame Loisel seemed depressed and dissatisfied.

"What is the matter?" asked her husband one evening. "You haven't been at all yourself the last three days."

She answered, "It vexes me to think that I haven't any jewellery to wear, not even a brooch. I shall feel like a perfect pauper. I would almost rather not go to the party."

"You can wear some fresh flowers. They are very fashionable this year. For ten francs you can get two or three spelndid roses."

She was not convinced.

"No, there is nothing more humiliating than to have an air of poverty among a crowd of rich women."

"How silly you are !" exclaimed her husband. "Why don't you ask your friend, Madame Forestier, to lend you some jewellery ? You know her quite well enough for that."

She uttered a cry of joy.

"Yes, of course, it never occurred to me."

The next day she paid her friend a visit and explained her predicament..

Madame Forestier went to her wardrobe, took out a large jewel-case and placed it open before her friend.

"Help yourself, my dear."

Madame Loisel saw some bracelets, a pearl necklace, a Venetian cross exquisitely worked in gold and jewels. She tried on these ornaments in front of the mirror and hesitated, reluctant to take them off and gived them back.

"Have you nothing else?" she kept asking.

"O yes, look for yourself. I don't know what you would prefer."

At length she discovered a black satin-case containing a superb diamond necklace, and her heart began to beat with frantic desire. With trembling hands she took it out, fastened it over her high-necked gown, and stood gazing at herself in rapture.

Then in an agony of doubt, she said :

"Will you lend me this? I shouldn't want anything else."

"Yes, certainly."

She threw her arms round her friend's neck kissed her effusively, and then fled with her treasure.

It was the night of the reception. Madame Loisel's triumph was complete. All smiles and graciousness, in her exquisite gown, she was the prettiest woman in the room. Her head was in a whirl of joy. The men stared at her and inquired her name and begged for an introduction, while the junior staff asked her for waltzes. She even attracted the attention of the minister himself.

Carried away by her enjoyment, glorying in her beauty and her success, she threw herself ecstatically into the dance. She moved as in a beatific dream, wherein were mingled all the homage and admiration she had evoked, all the desires she had kindled, all the complete and perfect triumph so dear to a woman's heart.

It was close on four before she could tear herself away. Ever since midnight her husband had been dozing in a little, deserted drawing-room together with three other men whose wives were enjoying themselves immensely.

He threw her outdoor wraps round her shoulders—unpretentious, everyday garments, whose shabbiness contrasted strangely with the elegance of her ball dress. Conscious of the incongruity, she was eager to be gone, in order to escape the notice of the other women in their luxurious furs. Loisel tried to restrain her.

"Wait here while I fetch a cab. You will catch cold outside."

But she would not listen to him, and hurried down the staircase. They went out into the street, but there was no cab to be seen. They continued their search, vainly hailing drivers whom they caught sight of in the distance. Shivering with cold and in desperation, they made their way towards the Seine. At last, on the quay, they found one of those old vehicles which are only seen in Paris after nightfall, as if ashamed to display their shabbiness by daylight.

The cab took them to their door in the Rue des Martyrs, and they gloomily climbed the stairs to their dwelling. All was over for her. As for him, he was thinking that he would have to be in the office by ten o'clock.

She took off her wraps in front of the mirror, for the sake of one last glance at herself in all her glory. But suddenly she uttered a cry. The diamonds were no longer, round her neck.

"What is the matter," asked her husband, who was already half undressed.

She turned to him in horror. "I .... I .... have lost Madame Forestier's necklace."

He started in dismay. "What? Lost the necklace? Impossible."

They searched the plaits of the gown, the folds of the cloak and all the pockets, but in vain.

"You are sure you had it on when you came away from the ball?"

"Yes, I remember feeling it in the lobby at the Education Office."

"But if you had lost it in the street, we should have heard it drop. It must be in the cab."

"Yes, I expect it is. Did you take the number?"

"No. Did you?"

"No."

They gazed at each other, utterly appalled. In the end Loisel put on his clothes again.

"I will go over the ground that we covered on foot and see if I cannot find it."

He left the house. Lacking the strength to go to bed, unable to think, she collapsed into a chair and remained there in her evening gown, without a fire.

About seven o'clock her husband returned. He had not found the diamonds.

He applied to the police; advertised a reward in the newspapers, made inquiries of all the hackney-cab officers; he visited every place that seemed to hold out a vestige of hope.

His wife waited all day long in the same distracted condition, overwhelmed by this appalling calamity.

Loisel returned home in the evening pale and hollow-cheeked. His efforts had been in vain.

"You must write to your friend." He said, "and tell her that you have broken the catch of the necklace and that you are having it mended. That will give us time to think things over."

She wrote a letter to his dictation.

* * * * *

After a week had elapsed, they gave up all hope. Loisel, who looked five years older, said:

"We must take steps to replace the diamonds."

On the following day they took the empty case to the jeweller whose name was inside the lid. He consulted his books.

"The necklace was not bought here, Madam. I can only have supplied the case."

They went from jeweller, to jeweller, in an endeavour to find a necklace, exactly like the one they had lost, comparing their recollections. Both of them were ill with grief and despair.

At last in a shop in the Palais Royal they found a diamond necklace which seemed to them exactly like the other. Its price was forty thousand francs. The jeweller agreed to sell it to them for thirty-six. They begged him not to dispose of it for three days, and they stipulated for the right to sell it back for thirty-four thousand francs, if the original necklace was found before the end of February.

Loisel had eighteen thousand francs left to him by his father, the balance of the sum he proposed to borrow. He raised loans in all quarters, a thousand francs from one man, five hundred from another, five louis here, three louis there. He gave promissory notes, agreed to exorbitant terms, had dealings with usurers, and with all the money-lending-hordes. He compromised his whole future, and had to risk his signature, hardly knowing if he would be able to honour it. Overwhelmed by the prospect of future suffering, the black misery which was about to come upon him, the physical privations and moral torments, he went to fetch the new necklace and laid his thirty-six thousands francs down on the jeweller's counter.

When Madame Loisel brought back the necklace, Madame Forestier said reproachfully:

"You ought to have returned it sooner; I might have wanted to wear it."

To madame Loisel's relief she did not open the case. Supposing she had noticed the exchange, what would she have thought? What would she have said? Perhaps she would have taken her for a thief.

* * * * *

Madame Loisel now became acquainted with the horrors of extreme poverty. She made up her mind to it, and played her part heroically. This appalling debt had to be paid, and pay it she would. The maid was dismissed; the flat, was given up, and they moved to a garret. She undertook all the rough household work and the odious duties of the kitchen. She washed up after meals and ruined her pink finger-nails scrubbing greasy dishes and saucepans. She washed the linen, the shirts and the dusters, and hung them out on the line to dry. Every morning she carried down the sweepings to the street, and brought up the water, pausing for breath at each landing. Dressed like a working woman, she went with her basket on her arm to the greengrocer, the grocer and the butcher, bargaining, wrangling and fighting for every farthing.

Each month some of the promissory notes had to be redeemed, and others renewed in order to gain time.

Her husband spent his evenings working at some tradesman's accounts and at night he would often copy papers at five sous a page.

This existence went on for ten years.

At the end of that time they had paid off everything to the last penny, including the usurious rates and the accumulations of interest.

Madame Loisel now looked an old woman. She had become the typical poor man's wife, rough, coarse, hard-bitten. Her hair was neglected, her skirts hung awry; and her hands were red. Her voice was no longer gentle, and she washed down the floors vigorously. But now and then, when her husband was at the office, she would sit by the window, and her thoughts would wander back to that far-away evening, the evening of her beauty and her triumph.

What would have been the end of it if she had not lost the necklace? Who could say? How strange, how variable are the chances of life! How small a thing can serve to save or ruin you!

One Sunday she went for a stroll in the Champs Elysees, for the sake of relaxation after the week's work, and she caught sight of a lady with a child. She recognised Madame Forestier who looked as young, as pretty, and as attractive as ever. Madame Loisel felt a thrill of emotion. Should she speak to her? Why not? Now that the debt was paid, why should she not tell her the whole story? She went up to her.

"Good morning, Jeanne."

Her friend did not recognize her and was surprised at being addressed so familiarly by this homely person.

"I am afraid I do not know you—you must have made a mistake," she said hesitatingly.

"No. I am Matilda Loisel."

Her friend uttered a cry.

"O my poor, dear Matilda, how you have changed."

"Yes, I have been through a very hard time since I saw you last; no end of trouble, and all through you."

"Through me? What do you mean?"

"You remember the diamond necklace you lent me to wear at the reception at the Education Office?"

"Yes. Well?"

"Well, I lost it."

"I don't understand; you brought it back to me."

"What I brought to you was another one, exactly like it. And for the last ten years we have been paying for it. You will understand that it was not an easy matter for people like us, who hadn't a penny. However, it's all over now. I can't tell you what a relief it is."

Madame Forestier stopped dead.

"You mean to say that you bought a diamond necklace to replace mine?"

"Yes. And you never noticed it? They were certainly very much alike."

She smiled with ingenuous pride and satisfaction.

Madame Forestier seized both her hands in great distress.

"O my poor, dear Matilda. Why, mine were only imitation. At the most they were worth five hundred francs!"

□

2. THE LAST LEAF

(O. Henry)

1. In a little district west of Washington Square the streets have run crazy and broken themselves into small strips called 'places'. These 'places' make strange angles and curves. One street crosses itself a time or two. An artist once discovered a valuable possibility in this street. Suppose a collector with a bill for paints, paper and canvas should, in traversing this route, suddenly meet himself coming back, without a cent having been paid on account!

2. So, to quaint old Greenwich Village the art people soon came prowling, hunting for north windows and eighteenth-century gables and Dutch attics and low rents. Then they imported some pewter mugs and a chafing dish or two from Sixth Avenue, and become a 'colony'.

3. At the top of a squatty, three-storey block, Sue and Johnsy had their studio. 'Johnsy' was familiar for Joanna. One was from Maine; the other from California. They had met at the table d'hote of an Eighth Street 'Delmonico's, and found their tastes in art, chicory, salad and bishop sleeves so congenial that the joint studio resulted.

4. That was in May. In November a cold, unseen stranger, whom the doctors called Pneumonia, stalked about the colony, touching one here and there with his icy finger. Over on the east side this ravager strode boldly, smiting his victims by scores, but his feet trod slowly through the maze of the narrow and moss-grown 'places'.

5. Mr. Pneumonia was not what you would call a chivalric old gentleman. A mite of a little woman with blood thinned by California zephyrs was hardly fair game for the red-fisted, short-breathed old duffer. But Johnsy he smote; and she lay, scarcely moving, on her painted iron bedstead, looking through the small Dutch window-panes at the blank side of the next brick house.

6. One morning the busy doctor invited Sue into the hallway with a shaggy, grey eyebrow.

'She has one chance in, let us say, ten', he said, as he shook down the mercury in his clinical thermometer. 'And that chance is for her to want to live. This way people have of lining up on the side of the undertaker makes the entire pharmacopoeia look silly. Your little lady has made up her mind that she's not going to get well. Has she anything on her mind?' 'She—she wanted to paint the Bay of Naples some day', said Sue.

'Paint?—bosh! Has she anything on her mind worth thinking about twice—a man, for instance?'

'A man?' said Sue, with a jew's-harp twang in her voice. 'Is a man worth—but, no, doctor there is nothing of the kind.'

7. 'Well. it is the weakness, then', said the doctor. 'I will do all that science, so far as it may filter through my efforts, can accomplish. But whenever my patient begins to count the carriages in her funeral procession I subtract 50 per cent from the curative power of medicines. If you will get her to ask one question about the new winter styles in clock sleeves I will promise you a one-in-five chance for her, instead of one-in-ten.'

8. After the doctor had gone, Sue went into the workroom and cried a Japanese napkin to a pulp. Then she swaggered into Johnsy's room with her drawing board, whistling ragtime.

Johnsy lay, scarcely making a ripple under the bed-clothes, with her face toward the window. Sue stopped whistling, thinking she was asleep.

9. She arranged her board and began a pen-and-ink drawing to illustrate a magazine story. Young artists must pave their way to Art by drawing pictures for magazine stories that young authors write to pave their way to literature.

As Sue was sketching a pair of elegant horse-show riding trousers and a monocle on the figure of the hero, an Idaho cowboy, she heard a low sound, several times repeated. She went quickly to the bedside.

10. Johnsy's eyes were wide open. She was looking out of the window and counting—counting backward.

'Twelve,' she said, and a little later, 'eleven', and then 'ten', and 'nine', and then 'eight' and 'seven' almost together.

11. Sue looked solicitously out of the window. What was there to count? There was only a bare dreary yard to be seen. and the blank side of the brick house twenty feet away. An old, old ivy vine, gnarled and decayed at the roots, climbed halfway up the brick wall. The cold breath of autumn had stricken its leaves from the vine until its skeleton branches clung, almost bare, to the crumbling bricks. 'What is it, dear?' asked Sue.

12. 'Six', said Johnsy, in almost a whisper. 'They're falling faster now. Three days ago there were almost a hundred. It made my head ache to count them. But now it's easy. There goes another one. There are only five left now.'

'Five what, dear? Tell your Sudie.'

'Leaves. On the ivy vine. When the last one falls I must go too. I've known that for three years. Didn't the doctor tell you?'

13. 'Oh, I never heard of such nonsense.' complained Sue, with magnificent scorn. 'What have old ivy leaves to do with your getting well? And you used to love that vine so, you naughty girl. Don't be a goosey. Why, the doctor told me this morning that your chances for getting well real soon were—let's see exactly what he said—he said the chances were ten to one! Why, that's almost as good a chance as we have in New York when we ride on the street cars or walk past a new building. Try to take some broth now, and let Sudie go back to her drawing, so she can sell the editor man with it, and buy port wine for her sick child, and pork chops for her greedy self.'

14. 'You needn't get any more wine' said Johnsy, keeping her eyes fixed out the window. 'There goes another. No, I don't want any broth. That leaves just four. I want to see the last one fall before it gets dark. Then I'll go too.'

'Johnsy, dear,' said Sue, bending over her, 'will you promise me to keep your eyes closed and not look out the window until I am done working? I must hand those drawings in by tomorrow. I need the light, or I would draw the shade down.'

'Couldn't you draw in the other room?' asked Johnsy coldly.

'I'd rather be here by you,' said Sue. 'Besides, I don't want you to keep looking at those silly ivy leaves.'

15. 'Tell me as soon as you have finished.' said Johnsy closing her eyes and lying white and still as a fallen statue, 'because I want to see the last one fall. I'm tired of waiting. I'm tired of thinking. I want to turn loose my hold on everything. and go sailing down, down, just like one of those poor, tired leaves.'

'Try to sleep,' said Sue. 'I must call Behrman up to be my model for the old hermit miner. I'll not be gone a minute. Don't try to move till I come back.'

16. Old Behrman was a painter who lived on the ground floor beneath them. He was past sixty and had a Michael Angelo's Moses beard curling down from the head of a satyr along the body of an imp. Behrman was. failure in art. Forty years he had wielded the brush without getting near enough to touch the hem of his Mistress's robe. He had been always about to paint a msterpiece, but had never yet begun it. For several years he had painted nothing except now and then a daub in the line of commerce or advertising. He earned a little by serving as a model to those young artists in the colony who could not pay the price of a professional. He drank gin to excess and still talked of his coming masterpiece. For the rest he was a fierce little old man, who scoffed terribly at softness in any one, and who regarded himself as a special mastiff-in-waiting to protect the two young artists in the studio above.

17. Sue found Behrman smelling strongly of juniper berries in his dimly lighted den below. In one corner was a blank canvas on an easel

that had been waiting there for twenty-five years to receive the first line of the masterpiece. She told him of Johnsy's fancy, and how she feared she would, indeed, light and fragile as a leaf herself, float away when her slight hold upon the world grew weaker.

18. Old Behrman, with his red eyes plainly streaming, shouted his contempt and derision for such idiotic imaginings.

'Vass.' he cried. 'Is dere people in de world mit der foolishness to die because leafs dey drop off from a confounded vine? I hap not heard of such a thing. No, I vill not bose as a model for your fool hermit—dunderhead. Vy do you allow dot silly pusiness to come in der prain of her? Ach, dot poor little Miss Yohnsy.'

'She is very ill and weak,' said Sue, 'and the fever has left her mind morbid and full of strange fancies. Very well, Mr. Behrman. If you do not care to pose for me, you needn't. But I think you are a horrid old—old flibbertigibbet.'

19. 'You are just like a woman,' yelled Behrman. 'Who said I vill not bose? Go on. I come mit you. For half and hour I haf peen trying to say dot I am ready to bose. Gott! dis is not any blace in which one so goot as Miss Yohnsy shall lie sick. Some day I vill baint a masterpiece, and ve shall all go avay. Gott! Yes.'

20. Johnsy was sleeping when they went upstairs. Sue pulled the shade down to the window-sill and motioned Behrman into the other room in there they peered out the window fearfully at the ivy vine. Then they looked at each other for a moment without speaking. A persistent, cold rain was falling mingled with snow. Behrman, in his old blue shirt took his seat as the hermit miner on an upturned kettle for a rock.

When Sue awoke from an hour's sleep the next morning she found Johnsy, with dull, wide open eyes staring at the drawn green shade. 'Pull it up; I want to see,' she ordered in a whisper. Wearily Sue obeyed.

21. But, lo! after the beating rain and fierce gusts of wind that had endured through the livelong night, there yet stood out against the brick wall one ivy leaf. It was the last on the vine. Still dark green near its stem, but with its serrated edges tinged with the yellow of dissolution and decay, it hung bravely from a branch some twenty feet above the ground.

22. 'It is the last one,' said Johnsy. 'I thought it would surely fall during the night. I heard the wind. It will fall to-day, and I shall die at the same time.'

'Dear, dear!' said Sue, leaning her worn face down to the pillow; 'think of me, if you won't think of yourself. What would I do?'

23. But Johnsy did not answer. The lonesomest thing in all the world is a soul when it is making ready to go on its mysterious, far journey. The fancy seemed to possess her more strongly as one by one

the ties that bound her to friendship and to earth were loosed.

24. The day wore away, and even through the twilight they could see the lone ivy leaf clinging to its stem against the wall. And then, with the coming of the night the north wind was again loosed, while the rain still beat against the windows and pattered down from the low Dutch eaves.

25. When it was light enough Johnsy, the merciless, commanded that the shade be raised.

The ivy leaf was still there.

26. Johnsy lay for a long time looking at it. And then she called to Sue, who was stirring her chicken broth over the gas stove.

27. 'I've been a bad girl, Sudie,' said Johnsy. 'Something has made that last leaf stay there to show me how wicked I was. It is a sin to want to die. You may bring me a little broth now, and some milk with a little port in it, and—no; bring me a hand mirror first; and then pack some pillows about me, and I will sit up and watch you cook.'

28. An hour later she said, 'Sudie, some day I hope to paint the Bay of Naples.'

The doctor came in the afternoon and Sue had an excuse to go into the hallway as he left.

29. 'Even chances,' said the doctor, taking Sue's thin, shaking hand in his. 'With good nursing you will win. And now I must see another case I have downstairs. Behrman, his name is—some kind of an artist, I believe Pneumonia too. He is an old, weak man, and the attack is acute. There is no hope for him; but he goes to the hospital today to be made more comfortable.'

30. The next day the doctor said to Sue: 'She's out of danger. You've won. Nutrition and care now—that's all.'

31. And that afternoon Sue came to the bed where Johnsy lay, contentedly knitting a very blue and very useless woollen shoulder scarf, and put one arm around her, pillows and all.

'I have something to tell you, white mouse,' she said. 'Mr. Behrman died of pneumonia today in the hospital. He was ill only two days. The janitor found him on the morning of the first day in his room downstairs helpless with pain. His shoes and clothing were wet through and icy cold. They couldn't imagine where he had been on such a dreadful night. An then they found a lantern, still lighted, and a ladder that had been dragged from its place and some scattered brushes, and a palette with green and yellow colours mixed on it, and—look out the window, dear, at the last ivy-leaf on the wall. Didn't you wonder why it never fluttered or moved when the wind blew? Ah, darling, it's Behrman's masterpiece—he painted it there the night that the last leaf fell.'

□

3. A CUP OF TEA

(Katherine Mansfield)

Rosemary Fell was not exactly beautiful. No, you couldn't have called her beautiful. Pretty? Well, if you took her to pieces ...... But why be so cruel as to take anyone to pieces? She was young, brilliant, extremely modern, exquisitely well dressed, amazingly well read in the newest of the new books, and her parties were the most delicious mixture of the really important people and ...... artists–quaint creatures, discoveries of hers, some of them too terrifying for words, but others quite presentable and amusing.

Rosemary had been married two years. She had a duck of a boy. No, not Peter-Michael. And her husband absolutely adored her. They were rich, really rich, not just comfortably well off, which is odious and stuffy and sounds like one's grandparents. But if Rosemary wanted to shop she would go to Paris as you and I would go to Bond Street. If she wanted to buy flowers, the car pulled up at that perfect shop in Regent Street, and Rosemary inside the shop just gazed in her dazzled, rather exotic way, and said : 'I want those and those and those. Give me four bunches of those, And that jar of roses. Yes, I'll have all the roses in the jar. No, no lilac. I hate lilac. It's got no shape.' The attendant bowed and put the lilac out of sight, as though this was only too true; lilac was dreadfully shapeless. 'Give me those stumpy little tulips. Those red and white ones.' And she was followed to the car by a thin shop-girl staggering under an immense white paper armful that looked like a baby in long clothes ....

One winter afternoon she had been buying something in a little antique shop in Curzon Street. It was a shop she liked. For one thing, one usually had it to oneself. And then the man who kept it was ridiculously fond of serving her. He beamed whenever she came in. He clasped his hands; he was so gratified he could scarcely speak. Flattery, of course. All the same, there was something..... .

'You see, madam,' he would explain in his low respectful tones, 'I love my things. I would rather not part with them than sell them to someone who does not appreciate them, who has not that fine feeling which is so rare....' And, breathing deeply, he unrolled a tiny square of blue velvet and pressed it on the glass counter with his pale finger-tips.

Today it was a little box. He had been keeping it for her. He had shown it to nobody as yet. An exquisite little enamel box with a glaze so fine it looked as though it had been baked in cream. On the lid a minute creature stood under a flowery tree, and a more minute creature still had her arms round his neck. Her hat, really no bigger than a geranium petal, hung from a branch; it had green ribbons. And there was a pink cloud like a watchful cherub floating above their heads. Rosemary took her hands out of her long gloves. She always took off her gloves to examine such things. Yes, she liked it very much. She loved it; it was a great duck. She must have it. And, turning the creamy box, opening and shutting it, she couldn't help noticing how charming her hands were against the blue velvet. The shopman, in some dim cavern of his mind, may have dared to think so, too. For he took a pencil, leant over the counter, and his pale bloodless fingers crept timidly towards those rosy, flashing ones, as he murmured gently : 'If I may venture to point out to madam, the flowers on the little lady's bodice.'

'Charming!' Rosemary admired the flowers. But what was the price? For a moment the shopman did not seem to hear. Then a murmur reached her. 'Twenty-eight guineas, madam.'

'Twenty-eight guineas.' Rosemary gave no sign. She laid the little box down; she buttoned her gloves again. 'Twenty-eight guineas. Even if one is rich ... She looked vague. She stared at a plump tea-kettle like a plump hen above the shopman's head, and her voice was dreamy as she answered : 'Well, keep it for me–will you? I'll...'

But the shopman had already bowed as though keeping it for her was all any human being could ask. He would be willing, of course, to keep it for her for ever.

The discreet door shut with a click. She was outside on the step, gazing at the winter afternoon. Rain was falling, and with the rain it seemed the dark came too, spinning down like ashes. There was a cold bitter taste in the air, and the new-lighted lamps looked sad. Sad were the lights in the houses opposite. Dimly they burned as if regretting something. And people hurried by, hidden under their hateful umbrellas. Rosemary felt a strange pang. She pressed her muff against her breast; she wished she had the little box, too, to cling to. Of course, the car was there. She'd only to cross the pavement. But still she waited. There are moments, horrible moments in life, when one emerges from shelter and looks out, and it's awful. One oughtn't to give way to them. One ought to go home and have an extra-special tea. "But at the very instant of thinking that, a young girl, thin, dark, shadowy—where had she come from?—was standing at Rosemary's elbow and a voice like a sigh, almost like a sob, breathed : 'Madam, may I speak to you a moment?'

'Speak to me?' Rosemary turned. She saw a little battered

creature with enormous eyes, someone quite young, no older than herself, who clutched at her coat-collar with reddened hands, and shivered as though she had just come out of the water.

'M-madam,' stammered the voice. 'Would you let me have the price of a cup of tea?'

'A cup of tea?' There was something simple, sincere in that voice; it wasn't in the least the voice of a beggar. 'Then have you no money at all?' asked Rosemary.

'None, madam,' came the answer.

'How extraordinary!' Rosemary peered through the dusk, and the girl gazed back at her. How more than extraordinary! And suddenly it seemed to Rosemary such an adventure. It was like something out of a novel by Dostoevsky, this meeting in the dusk. Supposing she took the girl home? Supposing she did do one of those things she was always roading about or seeing on the stage, what would happen? It would be thrilling. And she heard herself saying afterwards to the amazement of her friends : 'I simply took her home with me,' as she stepped forward and said to that dim person beside her : 'Come home to tea with me.'

The girl drew back startled. She even stopped shivering for a moment. Rosemary put out a hand and touched her arm. 'I mean it,' she said, smiling. And she felt how simple and kind her smile was. 'Why won't you? Do. Come home with me now in my car and have tea.

'You—you don't mean it, madam,' said the girl, and there was pain in her voice.

'But I do,' cried Rosemary. 'I want you to. To please me. Come along.'

The girl put her fingers to her lips and her eyes devoured Rosemary. 'You're—you're not taking me to the police station?' she stammered.

'The police station!' Rosemary laughed out. 'Why should I be so cruel? No, I only want to make you warm and to hear—anything you care to tell me.'

Hungry people are easily led. The footman held the door of the car open, and a moment later they were skimming through the dusk.

'There!' said Rosemary. She had a feeling of triumph as she slipped her hand through the velvet strap. She could have said, 'Now I've got 'you,' as she gazed at the little captive she had netted. But of course she meant it kindly. Oh, more than kindly. She was going to prove to this girl that—wonderful things did happen in life, that—fairy godmothers were real, that—rich people had hearts, and that women *were* sisters. She turned impulsively, saying : 'Don't be frightened. After all, why shouldn't you come back with me? We're both women. If I'm the more fortunate, you ought to expect....'

But happily at that moment, for she didn't know how the sentence was going to end, the car stopped. The bell was rung, the door opened, and with a charming, protecting, almost embracing movement, Rosemary drew the other into the hall. Warmth, softness, light, a sweet scent, all those things so familiar to her she never even thought about them, she watched that other receive. It was fascinating. She was like the rich little girl in her nursery with all the cupboards to open, all the boxes to unpack.

'Come, come upstairs,' said Rosemary, longing to begin to be generous. 'Come up to my room.' And, besides, she wanted to spare this poor little thing from being stared at by the servants; she decided as they mounted the stairs she would not even ring for Jeanne, but take off her things by herself. The great thing was to be natural!

And 'There!' cried Rosemary again, as they reached her beautiful big bedroom with the curtains drawn, the fire leaping on her wonderful lacquer furniture, her gold cushions and the primrose and blue rugs.

The girl stood just inside the door; she seemed dazed. But Rosemary didn't mind that.

'Come and sit down,' she cried, dragging her big chair up to the fire, 'in this comfy chair. Come and get warm. You look so dreadfully cold.'

'I daren't, madam,' said the girl, and she edged backwards.

'Oh, please,'—Rosemary ran forward—'you mustn't be frightened, you mustn't really. Sit down and when I've taken off my things we shall go into the next room and have tea and be cosy. Why are you afraid?' And gently she half pushed the thin figure into its deep cradle.

But there was no answer. The girl stayed just as she had been put, with her hands by her sides and her mouth slightly open. To be quite sincere, she looked rather stupid. But Rosemary wouldn't acknowledge it. She leant over her, saying : 'Won't you take off your hat? Your pretty hair is all wet. And one is so much more comfortable without a hat, isn't one?'

'There was a whisper that sounded like 'Very good, madam,' and the crushed hat was taken off.

'And let me help you off with your coat, too,' said Rosemary.

The girl stood up. But she held on to the chair with one hand and let Rosemary pull. It was quite an effort. The other scarcely helped her at all. She seemed to stagger like a child, and the thought came and went through Rosemary's mind, that if people wanted helping they must respond a little, just a little, otherwise it became very difficult indeed. And what was she to do with the coat now? She left it on the floor, and the hat too. She was just going to take a cigarette off the mantelpiece when the girl said quickly, but so lightly and strangely : I'm very sorry, madam, but I'm going to faint. I shall go off, madam, if I don't have something.'

'Good heavens, how thoughtless I am!' Rosemary rushed to the bell.

'Tea! Tea at once! And some brandy immediately!'

The maid was gone again, but the girl almost cried out : 'No, I don't want brandy. I never drink brandy. It's a cup of tea I want, madam.' And she burst into tears.

It was a terrible and fascinating moment. Rosemary knelt beside her chair.

'Don't cry, poor little thing,' she said. 'Don't cry.' And she gave the other her lace handkerchief. She really was touched beyond words. She put her arm round those thin, bird-like shoulders.

Now at last the other forgot to be shy, forgot everything except that they were both women, and gasped out : 'I can't go on no longer like this. I can't bear it. I shall do away with myself. I cant't bear no more.'

'You shan't have to. I'll look after you. Don't cry any more. Don't you see what a good thing it was that you met me? We'll have tea and you'll tell me everything. And I shall arrange something I promise. *Do* stop crying. It's so exhausting. Please!'

The other did stop just in time for Rosemary to get up before the tea came. She had the table placed between them. She plied the poor little creature with everything, all the sandwiches, all the bread and butter, and every time her cup was empty she filled it with tea, cream and sugar. People always said sugar was so nourishing. As for herself she didn't eat; she smoked and looked away tactfully so that the other should not be shy.

And really the effect of that slight meal was marvellous. When the tea-table was carried away, a new being, a light, frail creature with tangled hair, dark lips, deep, lighted eyes, lay back in the big chair in a kind of sweet languor, looking at the blaze. Rosemary lit a fresh cigarette; it was time to begin.

'And when did you have your last meal?' she asked softly.

But at that moment the door-handle turned.

'Rosemary, may I come in?' It was Philip.

'Of course.'

He came in. 'Oh, I'm so sorry,' he said, and stopped and stared.

'It's quite all right,' said Rosemary, smiling. 'This is my friend, Miss—'

'Smith, madam,' said the languid figure, who was strangely still and unafraid.

'Smith,' said Rosemary. 'We are going to have a little talk.'

'Oh yes,' said Philip. 'Quite,' and his eye caught sight of the coat and hat on the floor. He came over to the fire and turned his back to it. 'It's a beastly afternoon,' he said curiously, still looking at that listless figure, looking at its hands and boots, and then at Rosemary again.

'Yes, isn't it?' said Rosemary enthusiastically, 'Vile.'

Philip smiled his charming smile. 'As a matter of fact,' said he, 'I wanted you to come into the library for a moment. Would you? Will Miss Smith excuse us?'

The big eyes were raised to him, but Rosemary answered for her : 'Of course she will.' And they went out of the room together.

'I say,' said Philip, when they were alone, 'Explain. Who is she? What does it all mean?'

Rosemary, laughing, leaned against the door and said : 'I picked her up in Curzon Street. Really. She's a real pick-up. She asked me for the price of a cup of tea, and I brought her home with me.'

'But what on earth are you going to do with her?' cried Philip.

'Be nice to her,' said Rosemary quickly. 'Be frightfully nice to her. Look after her. I don't know how. We haven't talked yet. But show her–treat her–make her feel–'

'My darling girl,' said Philip, 'you're quite mad, you know. It simply can't be done.'

'I knew you'd say that,' retorted Rosemary. 'Why not? I want to. Isn't that a reason? And besides, one's always reading about these things. I decided—'

'But,' said Philip slowly, and he cut the end of a cigar, 'she's so astonishingly pretty.'

'Pretty?' Rosemary was so surprised that she blushed. 'Do you think so? I—I hadn't thought about it.'

'Good Lord!' Philip struck a match. 'She's absolutely lovely. Look again, my child. I was bowled over when I came into your room just now. However ...... I think you're making a ghastly mistake. Sorry, darling, if I'm crude and all that. But let me know if Miss Smith is going to dine with us in time for me to look up *The Milliner's Gazette.*'

'You absurd creature!' said Rosemary, and she went out of the library, but not back to her bedroom. She went to her writing-room and sat down at her desk. Pretty! Absolutely lovely! Bowled over! Her heart beat like a heavy bell. Pretty! Lovely! She drew her cheque book towards her. But no cheques would be no use, of course. She opened a drawer and took out five pound notes, looked at them, put two back, and holding the three squeezed in her hand, she went back to her bedroom.

Half an hour later Philip was still in the library, when Rosemary came in.

'I only wanted to tell you,' said she, and she leaned against the door again and looked at him with her dazzled exotic gaze, 'Miss Smith won't dine with us tonight.'

Philip put down the paper. 'Oh, what's happened? Previous engagement?'

Rosemary came over and sat down on his knee. 'She insisted on going,' said she, 'so I gave the poor little thing a present of money. I couldn't keep her against her will, could I?' she added softly.

Rosemary had just done her hair, darkened her eyes a little! and put on her pearls. She put up her hands and touched Philip's cheeks.

'Do you like me?' said she, and her tone, sweet, husky, troubled him.

'I like you awfully,' he said, and he held her tighter. 'Kiss me."

There was a pause.

Then Rosemary said dreamily : 'I saw a fascinating little box today. It cost twenty-eight guineas. May I have it?'

Philip jumped her on his knee. 'You may, little wasteful one,' said he.

But that was not really what Rosemary wanted to say.

'Philip,' she whispered, and she pressed his head against her bosom, 'am I *pretty*?'

□

4. THE LOST CHILD

(Mulk Raj Anand)

It was the festival of spring. From the wintry shades of narrow lanes and alleys emerged a gaily clad humanity, thick as a swarm of bright-coloured rabbits issuing from a warren. They entered the flooded sea of sparkling silver sunshine outside the city gates and sped towards the fair. Some walked, some rode on horses, others sat, being carried in bamboo and bullock carts. One little boy ran between his parent's legs, brimming over with life and laughter. The joyous morning gave greetings and unashamed invitations to all to come away into the fields, full of flowers and songs.

'Come, child, come,' called his parents, as he lagged behind, arrested by the toys in the shops that lined the way.

He hurried towards his parents, his feet obedient to their call, his eyes still lingering on the receding toys. As he came to where they had stopped to wait for him he could not suppress the desire of his heart, even though he well knew the old, cold stare of refusal in their eyes.

'I want that toy,' he pleaded.

His father looked at him red-eyed, in his familiar tyrant's way. His mother, melted by the free spirit of the day, was tender, and giving him her finger to catch, said : "Look, child, what is before you.'

The faint disgust of the child's unfulfilled desire had hardly been quelled in the heavy, pouting sob of a breath, 'm-o-th-er,' when the pleasure of what was before him filled his eager eye. They had left the dusty road on which they had walked so far. It wended its weary way circuitously to the north. They had come upon a footpath in a field.

It was a bowering mustard field, pale like melting gold as it swept across miles and and miles of even land—a river of yellow liquid light, ebbing and falling with each fresh eddy of wild wind, and straying in places into broad rich tributary streams, yet running in a constant sunny sweep towards the distant mirage of an ocean of silver light. Where it ended, on one side stood a cluster of low, mud-walled houses, thrown into relief by a dense crowed of yellow-robed men and women from which arose a high-pitched sequence of whistling, creaking, squeaking, roaring, humming noises, sweeping across the groves to the blue-throated sky like the weird, strange sound of Siva's mad laughter.

The child looked up to his father and mother, saturated with the shrill joy and wonder of this vast glory, and feeling that they, too, wore the evidence of this pure delight in their faces, he left the footpath and plunged headlong into the field, prancing like a young colt, his small feet timing with the fitful gusts of wind that came rich with the fragrance of more distant fields.

A group of dragon-flies were bustling about on their gaudy purple wings, intercepting the flight of a lone black butterfly in search of sweetness from the flowers. The child followed them in the air with his gaze, till one of them would fold its wings and rest, and he would try to catch it. But it would go fluttering, flapping, up into the air, when he had almost caught it in his hands. One bold back bee, having evaded capture, sought to tempt him by whining round his ear and nearly settled on his lips, when his mother gave a cautionary call : 'Come, child, come, come on to the footpath.'

He ran towards his parents gaily and walked abreast of them for a while, being, however, soon left behind, attracted by the little insects and worms along the footpath that were teeming out from their hiding-places to enjoy the sunshine.

'Come, child, come,' his parents called from the shade of a grove where they had seated themselves on the edge of a well. He ran towards them.

An old banyan here outstretched its powerful arms over the blossoming jack and *jaman* and neem and *champak* and *sirisha* and cast its shadows across beds of golden cassia and crimson gulmohur as an old grandmother spreads her skirts over her young ones. But the blushing blossoms freely offered their adoration to the Sun in spite of their protecting chaperon, by half covering themselves, and the sweet perfume of their pollen mingled with the soft, cool breeze that came and went in little puffs, only to be wafted aloft by a stronger breeze.

A shower of young flowers fell upon the child as he entered the grove and, forgetting his parents, he began to gather the raining petals in his hands. But lo! he heard the cooing of the doves and ran towards his parents, shouting : 'The dove! The dove!' The raining petals dropped from his forgotten hands. A curious look was in his parents' faces till a *koel* struck out a note of love and released their pent-up souls.

'Come, child, come!' they called to the child, who had now gone running in wild capers round the banyan tree, and gathering him up they took the narrow, winding footpath which led to the fair through the mustard fields.

As they neared the village the child could see many other footpaths full of throngs, converging to the whirlpool of the fair, and felt at once repelled and fascinated by the confusion of the world he was entering.

A sweetmeat-seller hawked: '*Gulab-jamun, rasgula, burfi, jalebi*', at the corner of the entrance, and a crowd pressed round his counter at the foot of an architecture of many-coloured sweets, decorated with leaves of silver and gold. The child stared open-eyed and his mouth watered for the *burfi* that was his favourite sweet. 'I want that *burfi*,' he slowly murmured. But he half knew as he begged that his plea would not be heeded because his parents would say he was greedy. So without waiting for an answer he moved on.

A flower-seller hawked : 'A garland of gulmohur, a garland of gulmohur.' The child seemed irresistibly drawn by the implacable sweetness of the scents that came floating on the wings of the languid air. He went towards the basket where the flowers were heaped and half murmured, 'I want that garland.' But he well knew his parents would refuse to buy him those flowers because they would say they were cheap. So without waiting for an answer he moved on.

A man stood holding a pole with yellow, red, green and purple balloons flying from it. The child was simply carried away by the rainbow glory of the silken colours and he was possessed by an overwhelming desire to possess them all. But he well knew his parents would never buy him the balloons because they would say he was too old to play with such toys. So he walked on farther.

A juggler stood playing a flute to a snake which coiled itself in a basket, its head raised in a graceful bend like the neck of a swan, while the music stole into its invisible ears like the gentle rippling of a miniature waterfall. The child went towards the juggler. But knowing his parents had forbidden him to hear such coarse music as the jugglers played, he proceeded farther.

There was a roundabout in full swing. Men, women and children, carried away in a whirling motion, shrieked and cried with his dizzy laughter. The child watched them intently going round and round, a pink blush of a smile on his face, his eyes rippling with the same movement, his lips parted in amazement, till he felt that he himself was being carried round. The ring seemed to go fiercely at first, then gradually it began to move less fast. Presently the child, rapt, finger in his mouth, beheld it stop. This time, before his overpowering love for the anticipated sensation of movement had been chilled by the thought of his parents, eternal denial, he made a bold request : 'I want to go on the roundabout, please, father, mother.'

There was no reply. He turned to look at his parents. They were not there, ahead of him. He turned to look on either side. They were not there. He looked behind. There was no sign of them.

A full, deep cry rose within his dry throat and with a sudden jerk of his body he ran from where he stood, crying in red fear, 'Mother, father. Tears rolled down from his eyes, hot and fierce; his flushed face was convulsed with fear. Panic-stricken, he ran to one side first, then to the other, hither and thither in all directions, knowing not where to go. 'Mother, father!' he wailed with a moist, shrill breath now, his throat being wet with swallowing the spittle. His yellow turban came untied and his clothes, wet with perspiration, became muddy where the dust had mixed with the sweat of his body. His light frame seemed heavy as a mass of lead.

Having run to and fro in a rage of running for a while he stood defeated, his cries suppressed into sobs. At little distances on the green grass he could see, through his filmy eyes, men and women talking. He tried to look intently among the patches of bright yellow clothes, but there was no sign of his father and mother among these people, who seemed to laugh and talk just for the sake of laughing and talking.

He ran hotly again, this time to a shrine to which people seemed to be crowding. Every little inch of space here was congested with men but he ran through people's legs, his little sob lingering 'Mother, father!' Near the entrance to the temple, however, the crowd became very thick : men jostled each other, heavy men, with flashing, murderous eyes and hefty shoulders. The poor child struggled to thrust a way between their feet but, knocked to and fro by their brutal movements, he might have been trampled underfoot had he not shrieked at the highest pitch of his voice : 'F-ather, mother!' A man in the surging crowd heard his cry and, stooping with very great difficulty, lifted him up in his arms.

'How did you get here, child? Whose baby are you?' the man asked as he steered clear of the mass. The child wept more bitterly than ever now and only cried : 'I want my mother, I want my father!'

The man tried to soothe him by taking him to the round about. 'Will you have a lift on the horse?' he gently asked as he approached the ring. The child's throat tore into a thousand shrill sobs and he only shouted : 'I want my mother, I want my father!'

The man headed towards the place where the juggler still played on the flute to the dancing cobra. 'Listen to that nice music, child,' he pleaded. But the child shut his ears with his fingers and shouted his double-pitched strain: 'I want my mother, I want my father!' The man took him near the balloons, thinking the bright colours of the balls would distract the child's attention and quieten him. 'Would you like a rainbow-coloured balloon?' he persuasively asked. 'The child turned his eyes from the flying balloons and just sobbed: 'I want my mother, I want my father.'

The man, still importunate in his kindly desire to make the child happy, bore him to the gate where the flower-seller sat. 'Look! Can you smell those nice flowers, child? Would you like a garland to put round your neck?' The child turned his nose away from the basket and reiterated his sob: 'I want my mother, I want my father.'

Thinking to humour his disconsolate charge by a gift of sweets, the man took him to the counter of sweet shop. 'What sweets would you like, child?' he asked. The child turned his face from the sweet shop and only sobbed. 'I want my mother, I want my father.'

□

5. THE BARBERS' TRADE UNION

(Mulk Raj Anand)

Among the makers of modern India, Chandu, the barber boy of our village, has a place which will be denied him unless I press for the recognition of his contribution to history. Chandu's peculiar claim to recognition rested, to tell the truth, on an exploit of which he did not know the full significance. But then, unlike most great men of India today, he had no very exaggerated notion of his own importance though he shared with them a certain naive egotism which was sometimes disconcerting and sometimes rather charming.

I knew Chandu ever since the days when he wore a piece of rag in the middle of his naked distended-bellied body, and when we wallowed together in the mire of the village lanes, playing at soldiering, shopkeeping, or clerking and other little games which we invented for the delectation of our two selves and of our mothers, who alone of all the elders condescended to notice us.

Chandu was my senior by about six months, and he always took the lead in all matters. And I willingly followed, because truly he was a genius at catching wasps, and at pressing the poison out of their tails, at tying their tiny legs to cotton thread and flying them, while I always got stung on the cheeks if I dared to go anywhere near the platform of the village well where these insects settled on the puddles to drink water.

When we grew up he still seemed to me the embodiment of perfection, because he could make and fly paper kites of such intricate design and of such balance as I could never achieve.

To be sure, he was not so good at doing sums at school as I was, perhaps because his father apprenticed him early to the hereditary profession of the barber's caste and sent him out hair-cutting in the village, and he had no time for the home tasks which our schoolmaster gave us. But he was better than I at reciting poetry, any day. For not only did he remember by rote the verses in the text book, but he could repeat the endless pages of prose in that book so that they seemed like poetry.

My mother resented the fact that Chandu won a scholarship at school while I had to pay fees to be taught. And she constantly dissuaded me from playing with him, saying that Chandu was a low caste barber's son and that I ought to keep up the status of my caste and class. But whatever innate ideas I had inherited from my forefathers, I certainly hadn't inherited any sense of supriority. Indeed I was always rather ashamed of the red caste mark which my mother put on my forehead every morning, and of the formalised pattern of the uchkin, the tight cotton trousers, the gold-worked shoes and the silk turban in which I dressed; and I longed for the right to wear all the spectacular conglomeration of clothes which Chandu wore—a pair of khaki shorts which the retired Subedar had given him, a frayed black velvet waistcoat, decorated all over with shell buttons, and a round felt cap which had once belonged to Lalla Hukam Chand, the lawyer of our village.

And I envied Chandu the freedom of movement which he enjoyed after his father died of plague. For then he would do the round of shaving and hair-cutting at the houses of the high-caste notables in the morning, bathe and dress, and then steal a ride to town, six miles away, on the footrest of the closed carriage in which Lalla Hukam Chand travelled to town.

Chandu was kind to me. He knew that I was seldom taken to town, and that I had to trudge three weary miles to a secondary school in the big village of Joadiala with the fear of God in my heart, while he had been completely absolved from the ordeal of being flogged by cruel masters as he had left school after his father's death. So he always brought me some gift or other from the town—a paint brush, or gold ink, or white chalk, or a double-edged penknife to sharpen pencils with; and he would entertain me with long merry descriptions of the variety of things he saw in the bazaars of civilization.

He was particularly detailed in his description of the wonderful English styles in clothes which he saw the Sahibs and the lawyers, the chaprasis and the policemen wearing at the District Court, where he had to wait for the journey home at the back of Lalla Hukam Chand's phaeton. And, once or twice, he expressed to me a secret wish he had to steal some money from the pitcher where his mother kept the emoluments of his professional skill, to buy himself a rig-out like that of Kalan Khan, the dentist, who, he said, performed miracles in the town, fitting people with rows of teeth and even new eyes. He described to me the appearance of Kalan Khan, a young man with hair parted on one side, and dressed in a starched shirt, with an ivory collar and bow tie, a black coat and striped trousers, and wonderful rubber overcoat and pumps. And he recounted to me the skill with which this magician unpaked an Angrezi leather handbag and flourished his shining steel instruments.

Then he asked my advice on the question of whether, as a barber educated to the fifth primary class, he would not look more dignified if he, too, wore a dress in the style of Dr. Kalan Khan, 'for though I am not a highly educated doctor,' he said, 'I learnt how to treat pimples, boils and cuts on people's bodies from my father, who learnt them from his father before him.'

I agreed with his project and encouraged him with the enthusiasm I felt for everything that my hero thought or did.

One day I was thrilled to find Chandu at the door of my house in the morning. He was dressed up in a white turban, a white rubber coat (a little too big for him, never the less very splendid), a pair of pumps in which I could see my face reflected in clear silhouette, and he had a leather bag in his hand. He was setting off on his round and had come to show me how grand he looked in his new rig-out.

'Marvellous!' I said, 'Marvellous!'

And he rushed off towards the house of the landlord, whom he shaved every morning, myself following admiringly behind.

There were not many people in the street at this time. So I alone witnessed the glory of Chandu, dressed up as a doctor, except, of course, that he himself seemed rather self-conscious as he strutted up the street, carefully avoiding the taint of cow-dung cakes which the village women struck to the walls, and the dirty water which flowed through the drains. But as we entered the home of the landlord we met Devi, the landlord's little son, who clapped his hands with joy and shouted to announce the coming of Chandu, the barber, in a beautiful heroic dress like that of Padre Sahib of the Mission School.

'Ram! Ram! Ram!' said Bijay Chand, the burly landlord, touching the sacred thread which hung over his ear since he had just been to the lavatory. 'The son of a pig! He is bringing a leather bag of cow-hide into our house and a coat of the marrow of, I don't know, some other animal, and those evil black Angrezi shoes. Get out! You son of a devil! You will defile my religion. I suppose you have no fear of anyone now that your father is dead!'

'But I am wearing the clothes of a Doctor, Jagirdar Sahib,' said Chandu.

'Go away you, swine, go away and wear clothes befitting your low status as a barber, and don't let me see you practising any of your new-fangled notions, or else I will have you flogged.

'But Rai Bijay Chand Sahib!' Chandu appealed.

'Get away! Get away! You useless one!' the landlord shouted. 'Don't come any nearer, or we will have to treat the whole house with the sacred cow-dung to purify it.'

Chandu returned. His face was flushed. He was completely taken aback. He did not look at me because of the shame he felt at being insulted before me whose hero he knew he was. And he rushed towards the shop of Thanu Ram, the Sahukar of the village, who kept a grocer's store at the corner of the lane.

Devi, the landlord's son, had begun to cry at his father's harsh words, and I stopped to quieten him. When I got to the head of the land I saw the Sahukar with one end of the scale in which he had been weighing grain lifted in one hand, abusing Chandu in the foulest way. 'You little swine, you go disguising yourself as a clown when you ought to be bearing your responsibilities and looking after your old mother. You go wearing the defiled clothes of the hospital folk! Go, and come back in your own clothes! Then I shall let you cut my hair! And as he said so he felt for the ritual tuft knot on top of his head. Chandu looked very crestfallen, and ran in a wild rage past me, as if I had been responsible for these mishaps. And I nearly cried to think that he hated me now just because I belonged to a superior caste.

'Go to Pandit Parmanand!' I shouted after him, 'and tell him that these garments you are wearing are not unclean.'

'Ho, so you are league with him,' said Pandit Parmanand, emerging from the landlord's home where he had been apparently summoned to discuss this unholy emergency. 'You boys have been spoiled by the school education which you have got. It may be all right for you to wear those things because you are going to be a learned man, but what right has that low-caste boy to such apparel? He has got to touch our beards, our heads and our hands. He is defiled enough by God. Why does he want to become more defiled? You are a high-caste boy. And he is low-caste devil! He is a rogue!'

Chandu had heard this. He did not look back but ran away.

My mother called to me and said it was time for me to eat and go to school, or I should be late. And she could not resist the temptation to lecture me again about my association with the barber boy.

But I was very disturbed about Chandu's fate all day, and, on my way back from school, I called in at the hovel where he lived with his mother.

His mother was well known for a cantankerous old woman, because she, a low-caste woman, dared to see the upper caste people as they never dared to see themselves. She was always very kind to me, though she spoke to me too in a bantering manner, which she had acquired through the suffering and humiliations of sixty-old years. Turning to me she said : 'Well, you have come, have you, to look for your friend. If your mother knew that you were here she would scratch my eyes out for casting my evil eye on your sweet face. And you, are you as innocent as you look or are you a sneaking little hypocrite like the rest of your lot?'

'Where is Chandu, then, mother?' I said.

'I don't know, son,' she said, now in a sincere simple manner. 'He went up town way and says he earned some money shaving people on the roadside. I don't know what he is up to. I don't think he ought to annoy the clients his father served. He is a child and gets funny notions into his head and they ought not to be angry with him. He is only a boy. You want to see him and go out playing. I suppose, Very well, I will tell him when he comes. He has just gone up the road, I think!'

'All right, mother,' I said and went home.

Chandu whistled for me that afternoon in the usual code whistle which we had arranged to evade the reproaches of interfering elders that our association often provoked.

'Come for a walk to the bazzar,' he said. 'I want to talk to you.' And hardly had I joined him when he began: 'Do you know, I earned a rupee shaving and hair cutting near the court this morning. If I hadn't had to come back on the back bar of Hukam Chand's carriage early in the afternoon, I should have earned more. But I am going to teach these orthodox idiots a lesson. I am going on strike. I shall not go to their houses to attend to them. I am going to buy a Japanese bicycle from the gambling son of Lalla Hukam Chand for five rupees, and I shall learn to ride it and I will go to town on it every day. Won't I look grand, riding on a bicycle, with my overcoat, my black leather shoes, and a white turban on my head, specially as there is a peg in front of the two-wheeled carriage for hanging my tool-bag?'

'Yes,' I agreed, greatly thrilled, not because I imagined the glory of Chandu seated on a bicycle, but because I felt myself nearer the goal of my own ambition; since I felt that if Chandu acquired a bicycle he would at least let me ride to town on the elongated bolt at the back wheel or on the front bar, if he didn't let me learn to ride myself and lend me the machine every now and then.

Chandu negotiated the deal about the bicycle with an assurance that seemed to me a revelation of his capacity for business such as I had never suspected in him, from the reckless way he spent his money. And then he said to me in a confidential voice: 'You wait for another day or two. I shall show you something which will make you laugh as you have never laughed before.'

'Tell me now,' I insisted, with an impatience sharpened by the rhythm of the excitement with which the spirit of his adventure filled my being.

'No, you wait,' he said. 'I can only give you a hint at the moment. It is a secret that only a barber can know. Now let me get on with the job of learning to handle this machine. You hold it while I get on it, and I think it will be all right.'

'But,' I said, 'this is not the way to learn to ride a bicycle. My father learned to ride from the peg at the back, and my brother learnt to ride by first trying to balance on the pedal.'

'Your father is a top-heavy baboon!' said Chandu, 'And your brother is a long-legged spider.'

'I', he continued, 'was born, my mother tells me, upside down.'

'All right,' I said, and I held the bicycle for him. But while my gaze concentrated with admiration on the brilliant sheen of the polished bars, I lost my grip and Chandu fell on the other side with a thud, along with the machine.

There were peals of laughter from the shop of the Sahukar, where several peasants congregated round the figure of the landlord. And then the Sahukar could be heard shouting: 'Serve you right, you rascally son of the iron age! Break your bones and die, you upstart! You won't come to your senses otherwise!'

Chandu hung his head with shame, and muttered an oath at me, 'You fool, you are no good!' though I had thought that he would grip me by the neck and give me a good thrashing for being the cause of his discomfiture. Then he looked at me, smiled embarrassedly, and said. 'We will see who has the last laugh, I or they.'

'I will hold the machin tightly this time,' I said earnestly, and I picked it up from where it let.

'Yes, break your bones, you swine,' came the landlord's call.

'Don't you care!' Chandu said to me. 'I will show them.' And he mounted the bicycle as I exerted all my strength to hold it tight. Then he said: 'Let go!' I released my grip.

He had pressed the pedal with a downward pressure of his right foot, hard, and, as the wheels revolved, he swayed dangerously to one side. But he had pushed the other pedal now. The machine balanced, inclining to the right a little, so that I saw Chandu lift his rump from the saddle in the most frightening manner. He hung precariously for a moment. His handles wobbled dangerously. He was tottering. At this juncture a mixed noise of laughter and sarcasm arose from the congregation at the shop and I thought that Chandu would come to grief with this confusion, if not on acount of his utter incapacity. By a curious miracle, however, Chandu's feet had got into the right rhythm for a pedalling and his handle had adjusted itself to his stiff hands, and he rode off with me running behind him, bursting myself with enthusiastic 'Shabashes.'

A half a mile run and he repeated the trick.

Though I was very eager to share the joy of his newly acquired skill, I didn't see Chandu the next day, as I was being taken to see my aunts in Verka, straight from school.

But on the third day he called for me and said that he would show me the joke he had talked of the other day.

I followed quickly, asked the while: 'Tell me, what is it all about?'

'Look,' he said, hiding behind the oven of the village, potter. 'Do you see the congregation of men in the Sahukar's shop? Try and see who's there.'

I explored the various faces, and for a moment, I was quite baffled.

'Only the peasants sitting round waiting for the landlord,' I said.

'Look again, idiot,' he said, 'and see. The landlord is there his long-jawed face dirtied by the white scum of his unshaved beard.'

'Ha! Ha!' I shouted hilariously, struck by the contradiction of the big thick moustache (which I knew the landlord dyed) with the prickly white bush on his jowls.

'Ha! Ha!' I shouted hilariously, struck by the contradiction of the big thick moustache (which I knew the landlord dyed) with the prickly white bush on his jowls.

'Ha! Ha!' I roared, 'a sick lion! He looks seedy!'

'Sh!' warned Chandu. 'Don't make a row! But look at the Sahukar. He looks like a leper with the brown tinge of tobacco on his walrus moustache which I once used to trim. Now you run past the shop and call 'Beavers, beavers!' They can't say anything to you!'

I was too impetuous a disciple of the impish Chandu to wait to deliberate.

'Beavers! Beavers! Beavers!' I shouted as I ran past the shop to the edge of the platform by the Banyan tree.

The peasants who were gathered round the shop burst out laughing, as they had apparently been itching to, for they had noticed the strong growths on the elder's faces, though they had not dared to say anything.

'Catch him, catch him, the little rogue!' shouted the Sahukar. 'He is in league with that barber boy, Chandu!'

But, of course, I had climbed up the Banyan tree, from which I jumped on to the wall of the temple and shouted my slogan at the priest.

The rumour about the barber boy's strike spread, and jokes about the unkempt beards of the elders of the village became current in every home. Even those who were of high castes, even the members of the families of the elders, began to giggle with laughter at the shabby appearance of the great ones and made rude remarks about their persons. And it was said that at least the landlord's wife threatened to run away with somebody, because, being younger than her husband by twenty years, she had borne with him as long as he kept himself in trim, but was now disgusted with him beyond the limits of reconciliation.

Chandu did good business in town during these days and saved money, even though he bought new clothes and new tools for himself and gave me various presents.

The village elders threatened to have him sent to prison for his offences, and ordered his mother to force him to obey before they committed him to the police for a breach of the peace.

But Chandu's mother had for the first time in her life touched the edge of prosperity, and she told them all what she thought of them in a language even plainer than that in which she had always addressed them.

Then they thought of getting the barber of Verka to come and attend them, and offered him an anna instead of the two pice they had usually paid to Chandu.

Chandu however, had conceived a new notion this time, newer than those he had ever thought of before. Having seen the shop of Nringan Das, the barber of the town, he had applied his brain to the scheme of opening a shop on the wayside at the head of the bazaar, in partnership with his cousin, the barber of Verka, and with Dhunoo and the other barbers within a range of seven miles from his village. He propsed his new idea to his cousin and Dhunoo and all the other barbers at a special meeting of his craft, and by that gift of the gab which he had, besides his other qualities of head and heart, he convinced them all that it was time that the elders of the village came to them to be shaved rather than they should dance attendance upon their lords and masters.

'Rajkot District Barber Brothers' Hairdressing and Shaving Saloon' has been followed by many other active trade unions of working men in our parts.

□

6. A HORSE AND TWO GOATS

(R. K. Narayan)

Of the seven hundred thousand villages dotting the map of India, in which the majority of India's five hundred million live, flourish, and die, Kritam was probably the tiniest, indicated on the district survey map by a microscopic dot, the map being meant more for the revenue official out to collect tax than for the guidance of the motorist, who is any case could not hope to reach it since it sprawled far from the highway at the end of a rough track furrowed up by the iron-hooped wheels of bullock carts. But its size did not prevent its giving itself the grandiose name Kritam, which meant in Tamil "coronet" or "crown" on the brow of this subcontinent. The village consisted of fewer than thirty houses, only one of them built with brick and cement. Painted a brilliant yellow and blue all over with gorgeous carvings of gods and gargoyles on its balustrade, it was known as the Big House. The other houses, distributed in four streets, were generally of bamboo thatch, straw, mud, and other unspecified material. Muni's was the last house in the fourth street, beyond which stretched the fields. In his prosperous days Muni had owned a flock of forty sheep and goats and sallied forth every morning driving the flock to the highway a couple of miles away. There he would sit on the pedestal of a clay statue of a horse while his cattle grazed around. He carried a crook at the end of a bamboo pole and snapped foliage from the avenue trees to feed his flock; he also gathered faggots and dry sticks, bundled them, and carried them home for fuel at sunset.

His wife lit the domestic fire at dawn, boiled water in a mud pot, threw into it a handful of millet flour, added salt, and gave him his first nourishment for the day. When he started out, she would put in his hand a packed lunch, once again the same millet cooked into a little ball, which he could swallow with a raw onion at midday. She was old, but he was older and needed all the attention she could give him in order to be kept alive.

His fortunes had declined gradually unnoticed. From a flock of forty which he drove into a pen at night, his stock had now come down to two goats, which were not worth the rent of a half rupee a month the Big House charged for the use of the pen in their backyard. And so the two goats were tethered to the trunk of a drumstick tree which grew in front of his hut and from which occasionally Muni could shake down drumsticks. This morning he got six. He carried them in with a sense of triumph. Although no one could say precisely who owned the tree, it was his because he lived in its shadow.

She said, "If you were content with the drumstick leaves alone, I could boil and salt some for you."

"Oh, I am tired of eating those leaves. I have a craving to chew the drumstick out of sauce, I tell you."

"You have only four teeth in your jaw, but your craving is for big things. All right, get the stuff for the sauce, and I will prepare it for you. After all, next year you may not be alive to ask for anything. But first get me all the stuff, including a measure of rice or millet, and I will satisfy your unholy craving. Our store is empty today. Dhall, chili, curry leaves, mustard, coriander, gingelley oil, and one large potato. Go out and get all this." He repeated the list after her in order not to miss any item and walked off to the shop in the third street.

He sat on an upturned packing case below the platform of the shop. The shopman paid no attention to him. Muni kept clearing his throat, coughing, and sneezing until the shopman could not stand it any more and demanded. "What ails you? You will fly off that seat into the gutter if you sneeze so hard, young man." Muni laughed inordinately, in order to please the shopman, at being called "young man." The shopman softened and said. "You have enough of the imp inside to keep a second wife busy, but for the fact the old lady is still alive." Muni laughed appropriately again at this joke. It completely won the shopman over he liked his sense of humour to be appreciated. Muni engaged his attention in local gossip for a few minutes, which always ended with a reference to the postman's wife, who had eloped to the city some months before.

The shopman felt most pleased to hear the worst of the postman, who had cheated him. Being an itinerant postman, he returned home to Kritam only once in ten days and every time managed to slip away again without passing the shop in the third street. By thus humouring the shopman, Muni could always ask for one or two items of food, promising repayment later. Some days the shopman was in a good mood and gave in, and sometimes he would lose his temper suddenly and bark at Muni for daring to ask for credit. This was such a day, and Muni could not progress beyond two items listed as essential components. The shopman was also displaying a remarkable memory for old facts and figures and took out an oblong ledger to support his observations. Muni felt impelled to rise and flee. But his self-respect kept him in his seat and made him listen to the worst things about himself. The shopman concluded, "If you could find five rupees and a quarter, you will have paid off an ancient debt and then could apply for admission to swarga. How much have you got now?"

"I will pay you everything on the first of the next month."

"As always, and whom do you expect to rob by then?"

Muni felt caught and mumbled, "My daughter has sent word that she will be sending me money."

"Have you a daughter?" sneered the shopman. "And she is sending you money! For what purpose, may I know?"

"Birthday, fiftieth birthday," said Muni quietly.

"Birthday! How old are you?"

Muni repeated weakly, not being sure of it himself, "Fifty." He always calculated his age from the time of the great famine when he stood as high as the parapet around the village well, but who could calculate such things accurately nowadays with so many famines occurring? The shopman felt encouraged when other customers stood around to watch and comment. Muni thought helplessly, My poverty is exposed to everybody. But what can I do?

"More likely you are seventy," said the shopman. "You also forget that you mentioned a birthday five weeks ago when you wanted castor oil for your holy bath."

"Bath! Who can dream of a bath when you have to scratch the tank-bed for a bowl of water? We would all be parched and dead but for the Big House, where they let us take a pot of water from their well." After saying this Muni unobtrusively rose and moved off.

He told his wife, "That scoundrel would not give me anything. So go out and sell the drumsticks for what they are worth."

He flung himself down in a corner to recoup from the fatigue of his visit to the shop. His wife said, "You are getting no sauce today, nor anything else. I can't find anything to give you to eat. Fast till the evening, it'll do you good. Take the goats and be gone now," she cried and added, "Don't come back before the sun is down." He knew that if he obeyed her she would somehow conjure up some food for him in the evening. Only he must be careful not to argue and irritate her. Her temper was undependable in the morning but improved by evening time. She was sure to go out and work—grind corn in the Big House, sweep or scrub somewhere, and earn enough to buy foodstuff and keep a dinner ready for him in the evening.

Unleashing the goats from the drumstick tree, Muni started out, driving them ahead and uttering weird cries from time to time in order to urge them on. He passed through the village with his head bowed in thought. He did not want to look at anyone or be accosted. A couple of cronies lounging in the temple corridor hailed him, but he ignored their call. They had known him in the days of affluence when he lorded over a flock of fleecy sheep, not the miserable gawky goats that he had today. Of course he also used to have a few goats for those who fancied them, but real wealth lay in sheep; they bred fast and people came and bought the fleece in the shearing season; and then that famous butcher from the town came over on the weekly market days bringing him betel leaves, tobacco, and often enough some bhang, which they smoked in a hut in the coconut grove, undisturbed by wives and well-wishers. After a smoke one felt light and elated and inclined to forgive everyone including that brother-in-law of his who had once tried to set fire to his home. But all this seemed like the memories of a previous birth. Some pestilence afflicted his cattle (he could of course guess who had laid his animals under a curse), and even the friendly butcher would not touch one at half the price ... and now here he was left with the two scraggy creatures. He wished someone would rid him of their company, too. The shopman had said that he was seventy. At seventy, one only waited to be summoned by God. When he was dead what would his wife do? They had lived in each other's company since they were children. He was told on their day of wedding that he was ten years old and she was eight. During the wedding ceremony they had had to recite their respective ages and names. He had thrashed her only a few times in their career, and later she had the upper hand. Progeny, none. Perhaps a large progeny would have brought him the blessing of the gods. Fertility brought merit. People with fourteen sons were always so prosperous and at peace with the world and themselves. He recollected the thrill he had felt when he mentioned a daughter to that shopman; although it was not believed, what if he did not have a daughter?—his cousin in the next village had many daughters, and any one of them was as good as his; he was fond of them all and would buy them sweets if he could afford it. Still, everyone in the village whispered behind their backs that Muni and his wife were a barren couple. He avoided looking at anyone; they all professed to be so high up, and everyone else in the village had more money than he. "I am the poorest fellow in our caste and no wonder that they spurn me, but I won't look at them either," and so he passed on with his eyes downcast along the edge of the street, and people left him also very much alone, commenting only to the extent, "Ah, there he goes with his two goats; if he slits their throats, he may have more peace of mind." "What has he to worry about anyway? They live on nothing and have none to worry about." Thus people commented when he passed through the village. Only on the outskirts did he lift his head and look up. He urged and bullied the goats until they meandered along to the foot of the horse statue on the edge of the village. He sat on its pedestal for the rest of the day. The advantage of this was that he could watch the highway and see the lorries and buses pass through to the hills, and it gave him a sense of belonging to a larger world. The pedestal of the statue was broad enough for him to move around as the sun travelled up and westward; or he could also crouch under the belly of the horse, for shade.

The horse was nearly life-size, moulded out of clay, baked, burnt, and brightly coloured, and reared its head proudly, prancing its forelegs in the air and flourishing its tail in a loop; beside the horse stood a warrior with scythe-like mustachios, bulging eyes, and aquiline nose. The old image-makers believed in indicating a man of strength by bulging out his eyes and sharpening his moustache tips, and also decorated the man's chest with beads which looked today like blobs of mud through the ravages of sun and wind and rain (when it came), but Muni would insist that he had known the beads to sparkle like the nine gems at one time in his life. The horse itself was said to have been as white as a dhobi-washed sheet, and had on its back a cover of pure brocade of red and black lace, matching the multicoloured sash around the waist of the warrior. But none in the village remembered the splendour as no one noticed its existence. Even Muni, who spent all his waking hours at its foot, never bothered to look up. It was untouched even by the young vandals of the village who gashed tree trunks with knives and tried to topple off milestones and inscribed lewd designs on all walls. This statue had been closer to the population of the village at one time, when this spot bordered the village; but when the highway was laid through (or perhaps when the tank and wells dried up completely here) the village moved a couple of miles inland.

Muni sat at the foot of the statue, watching his two goats graze in the arid soil among the cactus and lantana bushes. He looked at the sun; it was tilted westward no doubt, but it was not the time yet to go back home; if he went too early his wife would have no food for him. Also he must give her time to cool off her temper and feel sympathetic, and then she would scrounge and manage to get some food. He watched the mountain road for a time signal. get some food. He watched the mountain road for a time signal. When the green bus appeared around the bend he could leave and his wife would feel pleased that he had let the goats feed long enough.

He noticed now a new sort of vehicle coming down at full speed. It looked like both a motor car and a bus. He used to be intrigued by the novelty of such spectacles, but of late work was going on at the source of the river on the mountain and an assortment of people and traffic went past him, and he took it all casually and described to his wife, later in the day, everything he saw. Today, while he observed the yellow vehicle coming down, he was wondering how to describe it later to his wife, when it sputtered and stopped in front of him. A red-faced foreigner, who had been driving it, got down and went round it, stooping, looking, and poking under the vehicle; then he straightened himself up, looked at the dashboard, stared in Muni's direction, and approached him. "Excuse me, is there a gas station nearby, or do I have to wait until another car comes—" He suddenly looked up at the clay horse and cried, "Marvellous," without completing his sentence. Muni felt he should get up and run away, and cursed his age. He could not readily put his limbs into action; some years ago he could outrun a cheetah, as happened once when he went to the forest to cut fuel and it was then that two of his sheep were mauled—a sign that bad times were coming. Though he tried, he could not easily extricate himself from his seat, and then there was also the problem of the goats. He could not leave them behind.

The red-faced man wore khaki clothes—evidently a policeman or a soldier. Muni said to himself, He will chase or shoot if I start running. Some dogs chase only those who run—O Siva, protect me. I don't know why this man should be after me. Meanwhile the foreigner cried, "Marvellous!" again, nodding his head. He paced around the statue with his eyes fixed on it. Muni sat frozen for a while, and then fidgeted and tried to edge away. Now the other man suddenly pressed his palms together in a salute, smiled, and said, "Namaste! How do you do?"

At which Muni spoke the only English expressions he had learnt, "Yes, no." Having exhausted his English vocabulary, he started in Tamil: "My name is Muni. These two goats are mine, and no one can gainsay it—though our village is full of slanderers these days who will not hesitate to say that what belongs to a man doesn't belong to him." He rolled his eyes and shuddered at the thought of evil-minded men and women peopling his village.

The foreigner faithfully looked in the direction indicated by Muni's fingers, gazed for a while at the two goats and the rocks, and with a puzzled expression took out his silver cigarette case and lit a cigarette. Suddenly remembering the courtesies of the season, he asked, "Do you smoke?" Muni answered "Yes, no." Whereupon the red-faced man took a cigarette and gave it to Muni, who received it with surprise, having had no offer of a smoke from anyone for years now. Those days when he smoked bhang were gone with his sheep and the large-hearted butcher. Nowadays he was not able to find even matches, let alone bhang. (His wife went across and borrowed a fire at down from a neighbour.) He had always wanted to smoke cigarette; only once did the shopman give him one on credit, and he remembered how good it had tasted. The other flicked the lighter open and offered a light to Muni. Muni felt so confused about how to act that he blew on it and put it out. The other, puzzled but undaunted, flourished his lighter, presented it again, and lit Muni's cigarette. Muni drew a deep puff and started coughing; it was racking, no doubt, but extremely pleasant. When his cough subsided he wiped his eyes and took stock of the situation, understanding that the other man was not an Inquisitor of any kind. Yet, in order to make sure, he remained wary. No need to run away from a man who gave him such a potent smoke. His head was reeling from the effect of one of those strong American cigarettes made with roasted tobacco. The man said, "I come from New York," took out a wallet from his hip pocket, and presented his card.

Muni shrank away from the card. Perhaps he was trying to present a warrant and arrest him. Beware of khaki, one part of his mind warned. Take all the cigarettes or bhang or whatever is offered, but don't get caught. Beware of khaki. He wished he weren't seventy as the shopman had said. At seventy one didn't run, but surrendered to whatever came. He could only ward off trouble by talk. So he went on, all in the chaste Tamil for which Kritam was famous. (Even the worst detractors could not deny that the famous poetess Avaiyar was born in this area, although no one could say whether it was in Kritam or Kuppam, the adjoining village.) Out of this heritage the Tamil language gushed through Muni in an unimpeded flow. He said, "Before God, sir, Bhagwan, who sees everything, I tell you, sir, that we know nothing of the case. If the murder was committed, whoever did it will not escape. Bhagwan is all-seeing. Don't ask me about it. I know nothing." A body had been found mutilated and thrown under a tamarind tree at the border between Kritam and Kuppam a few weeks before, giving rise to much gossip and speculation. Muni added an explanation. "Anything is possible there. People over there will stop at nothing." The foreigner nodded his head and listened courteously thought he undetrstood nothing.

"I am sure you know when this horse was made," said the red man and smiled ingratiatingly.

Muni reacted to the relaxed atmosphere by smiling himself, and pleaded, "Please go away, sir, I know nothing. I promise we will hold him for you if we see any bad character around, and we will bury him up to his neck in a coconut pit if he tries to escape; but our village has always had a clean record. Must definitely be the other village."

Now the red man implored, "Please, please, I will speak slowly, please try to understand me, Can't you understand even a simple word of English? Everyone in this country seems to know English. I have gotten along with English everywhere in this country, but you don't speak it. Have you any religious or spiritual scruples against English speech?"

Muni made some indistinct sounds in his throat and shook his head. Encouraged, the other went on to explain at length, uttering each syllable with care and deliberation. Presently he sidled over and took a seat beside the old man, explaining, "You see, last August, we probably had the hottest summer in history, and I was working in shirt-sleeves in my office on the fortieth floor of the Empire State Building. We had a power failure one day, you know, and there I was stuck for four hours, no elevator, no air conditioning. All the way in the train I kept thinking, and the minute I reached home in Connecticut, I told my wife, Ruth, 'We will visit India this winter, it's time to look at other civilizations.' Next day she called the travel agent first thing and told him to fix it, and so here I am. Ruth came with me but is staying back at Srinagar, and I am the one doing the rounds and joining her later."

Muni looked reflective at the end of this long oration and said, rather feebly, "Yes, no," as a concession to the other's language, and went on in Tamil, "When I was this high"—he indicated a foot high—"I had heard my uncle say ..."

No one can tell what he was planning to say, as the other interrupted him at this stage to ask, "Boy, what is the secret of your teeth? How old are you?"

The old man forgot what he had started to say and remarked, "Sometimes we too lose our cattle. Jackals or cheetahs may sometimes carry them off, but sometimes it is just theft from over in the next village, and then we will know who has done it. Our priest at the temple can see in the camphor flame the face of the theif, and when he is caught ..." He gestured with his hands a perfect mincing of meat.

The American watched his hands intently and said, "I know what you mean. Chop something? Maybe I am holding you up and you want to chop wood? Where is your axe? Hand it to me and show me what to chop. I do enjoy it, you know, just a hobby. We get a lot of driftwood along the backwater near my house, and on Sundays I do nothing but chop wood for the fireplace. I really feel different when I watch the fire in the fireplace, although it may take all the sections of the Sunday *New York Times* to get a fire started." And he smiled at this reference.

Muni felt totally confused but decided the best thing would be to make an attempt to get away from this place. He tried to edge out, saying, "Must go home," and turned to go. The other seized his shoulder and said desperately, "Is there no one, absolutely no one here, to translate for me?" He looked up and down the road, which was deserted in this hot afternoon; a sudden gust of wind churned up the dust and dead leaves on the roadside into a ghostly column and propelled it towards the mountain road. The stranger almost pinioned Muni's back to the statue and asked, "Isn't this statue yours? Why don't you sell it to me?"

The old man now understood the reference to the horse, thought for a second, and said in his own language, "I was an urchin this high when I heard my grandfather explain this horse and warrior, and my grandfather himself was this high when he heard his grandfather, whose grandfather ..."

The other man interrupted him. "I don't want to seem to have stopped here for nothing. I will offer you a good price for this," he said, indicating the horse. He had concluded without the least doubt that Muni owned this mud horse. Perhaps he guessed by the way he sat on its pedestal, like other souvenir sellers in this country presiding over their wares.

Muni followed the man's eyes and pointing fingers and dimly understood the subject matter and, feeling relieved that the theme of the mutilated body had been abandoned at least for the time being, said again, enthusiastically, "I was this high when my grandfather told me about this horse and the warrior, and my grandfather was this high when he himself ..." and he was getting into a deeper bog of reminiscence each time he tried to indicate the antiquity of the statue.

The Tamil that Muni spoke was stimulating even as pure sound, and the foreigner listened with fascination. "I wish I had my tape-recorder here," he said, assuming the pleasantest expression. "Your language sounds wonderful. I get a kick out of every word you utter, here"—he indicated his ears—"but you don't have to waste your breath in sales talk. I appreciate the article. You don't have to explain its points."

"I never went to a school, in those days only Brahmin went to schools, but we had to go out and work in the fields morning till night, from sowing to harvest time ... and when Pongal came and we had cut the harvest my father allowed me to go out and play with others at the tank, and so I don't know the Parangi language you speak, even little fellows in your country probably speak the Parangi language, but here only learned men and officers know it. We had a postman in our village who could speak to you boldly in your language, but his wife ran away with someone and he does not speak to anyone at all nowadays. Who would if a wife did what she did? Women must be watched; otherwise they will sell themselves and the home." And he laughed at his own quip.

The foreigner laughed heartily, took out another cigarette, and offered it to Muni, who now smoked with ease, deciding to stay on if the fellow was going to be so good as to keep up his cigarette supply. The American now stood up on the pedestal in the attitude of a demonstrative lecturer and said, running his finger along some of the carved decorations around the horse's neck, speaking slowly and uttering his words syllable by syllable, "I could give a sales talk for this better than anyone else... This is a marvelous combination of yellow and indigo, though faded now ... How do you people of this country achieve these flaming colours?"

Muni, now assured that the subject was still the horse and not the dead body, said, "This is our guardian, it means death to our adversaries. At the end of Kali Yuga, this world and all other worlds will be destroyed, and the Redeemer will come in the shape of a horse called Kalki; this horse will come to life and gallop and trample down all bad men." As he spoke of bad men the figures of his shopman and his brother-in-law assumed concrete forms in his mind, and he revelled for a moment in the predicament of the fellow under the horse's hoof: served him right for trying to set fire to his home... .

While he was brooding on this pleasant vision, the foreigner utilized the pause to say, "I assure you that this will have the best home in the U.S.A. I'll push away the bookcase, you know I love books and am a member of five book clubs, and the choice and bonus volumes mount up to a pile really in our living room, as high as this horse itself. But they'll have to go. Ruth may disapprove, but I will convince her. The TV may have to be shifted, too. We can't have everything in the living room. Ruth will probably say what about when we have a party? I'm going to keep him right in the middle of the room. I don't see how that can interfere with the party—we'll stand around him and have our drinks."

Muni continued his description of the end of the world. "Our pundit discoursed at the temple once how the oceans are going to close over the earth in a huge wave and swallow us—this horse will grow bigger than the biggest wave and carry on its back only the good people and kick into the floods the evil ones—plenty of them about —" he said reflectively. "Do you know when it is going to happen?" he asked.

The foreigner now understood by the tone of the other that a question was being asked and said, "How am I transporting it? I can push the seat back and make room in the rear. That van can take in an elephant" —waving precisely at the back of the seat.

Muni was still hovering on visions of avatars and said again, "I never missed our pundit's discourses at the temple in those days during every bright half of the month, although he'd go on all night, and he told us that Vishnu is the highest god. Whenever evil men trouble us, he comes down to save us. He has come many times. The first time he incarnated as a great fish, and lifted the scriptures on his back when the flood and sea waves..."

"I am not a millionaire, but a modest businessman. My trade is coffee."

Amidst all this wilderness of obscure sound Muni caught the word "coffee" and said, "If you want to drink 'kapi,' drive further up, in the next town, they have Friday market and there they open 'kapi-otels'—so I learn from passers-by. Don't think I wander about. I go nowhere and look for nothing." His thoughts went back to the avatars. "The first avatar was in the shape of a little fish in a bowl of water, but every hour it grew bigger and bigger and became in the end a huge whale which the seas could not contain, and on the back of the whale the holy books were supported, saved, and carried." Once he had launched on the first avatar, it was inevitable that he should go on to the next, a wild boar on whose tusk the earth was lifted when a vicious conqueror of the earth carried it off and hid it at the bottom of the sea. After describing this avatar Muni concluded, "God will always save us whenever we are troubled by evil beings. When we were young we staged at full moon the story of the avatars. That's how I know the stories; we played them all night until the sun rose, and sometimes the European collector would come to watch, bringing his own chair. I had a good voice and so they always taught me songs and gave me the women's roles. I was always Goddess Lakshmi, and they dressed me in a brocade sari, loaned from the Big House ..."

The foreigner said, "I repeat I am not a millionaire. Ours is a modest business; after all, we can't afford to buy more than sixty minutes of TV time in a month, which works out to two minutes a day, that's all, although in the course of time we'll may be sponsor a one-hour show regularly if our sales graph continues to go up ..."

Muni was intoxicated by the memory of his theatrical days and was about to explain how he had painted his face and worn a wig and diamond earrings when the visitor, feeling that he had spent too much time already, said, "Tell me, will you accept a hundred rupees or not for the horse? I'd love to take the whiskered soldier also but no space for him this year. I'll have to cancel my air ticket and take a boat home, I suppose. Ruth can go by air if she likes, but I will go with the horse and keep him in my cabin all the way if necessary." And he smiled at the picture of himself voyaging across the seas hugging this horse. He added. "I will have to pad it with straw so that it doesn't break..."

"When we played *Ramayana,* they dressed me as Sita," added Muni. "A teacher came and taught us the songs for the drama and we gave him fifty rupees. He incarnated himself as Rama, and he alone could destroy Ravana, the demon with ten heads who shook all the worlds: do you know the story of *Ramayana?*"

"I have my station wagon as you see. I can push the seat back and take the horse in if you will just lend me a hand with it."

"Do you know *Mahabharata?* Krishna was the eighth avatar of Vishnu, incarnated to help the Five Brothers regain their kingdom. When Krishna was a baby he danced on the thousand-hooded giant serpent and trampled it to death; and then he suckled the breasts of the demoness and left them flat as a disc, though when she came to him her bosoms were large, like mounds of earth on the banks of a dug-up canal." He indicated two mounds with his hands.

The stranger was completely mystified by the gesture. For the first time he said, "I really wonder what you are saying because you answer is crucial. We have come to the point when we should be ready to talk business."

"When the tenth avatar comes, do you know where you and I will be?" asked the old man.

"Lend me a hand and I can lift off the horse from its pedestal after picking out the cement at the joints. We can do anything if we have a basis of understanding."

At this stage the mutual mystification was complete, and there was no need even to carry on a guessing game at the meaning of words. The old man chattered away in a spirit of balancing off the credits and debits of conversational exchange, and said in order to be on the credit sale, "Oh, honourable one, I hope God has blessed you with numerous progeny. I say this because you seem to be a good man, willing to stay beside an old man and talk to him, while all day I have none to talk to except when somebody stops by to ask for a piece of tobacco. But I seldom have it, tobacco is not what it used to be at one time, and I have given up chewing. I cannot afford it nowadays." Noting the other's interest in his speech, Muni felt encouraged to ask, "How many children have you?" with appropriate gestures with his hands.

Realizing that a question was being asked, the red man replied, "I said a hundred," which encouraged Muni to go into details. "How many of your children are boys and how many girls? Where are they? Is your daughter married? Is it difficult to find a son-in-law in your country also?"

In answer to these questions the red man dashed his hand into his pocket and brought forth his wallet in order to take immediate advantage of the bearish trend in the market. He flourished a hundred-rupee currency note and said, "Well, this is what I meant."

The old man now realized that some financial element was entering their talk. He peered closely at the currency note, the like of which he had never seen in his life; he knew the five and ten by their colours although always in other people's hands, while his own earning at any time was in coppers and nickels. What was this man flourishing the note for? Perhaps asking for change. He laughed to himself at the notion of anyone coming to him for changing a thousand- or ten-thousand-rupee note. He said with a grin, "Ask our village headman, who is also a money lender; he can change even a lakh of rupees in gold sovereigns if you prefer it that way; he thinks nobody knows, but dig the floor of his puja room and your head will reel at the sight of the hoard. The man disguises himself in rags just to mislead the public. Talk to the headman youself because he goes mad at the sight of me. Someone took away his pumpkins with the creeper and he, for some reason, thinks it was me and my goats ... that's why I never let my goats be seen anywhere near the farms." His eyes travelled to his goats nosing about, attempting to wrest nutrition from minute greenery peeping out of rock and dry earth.

The foreigner followed his look and decided that it would be a sound policy to show an interest in the old man's pets. He went up casually to them and stroked their backs with every show of courteous attention. Now the truth dawned on the old man. His dream of a lifetime was about to be realized. He understood that the red man was actually making an offer for the goats. He had reared them up in the hope of selling them some day and, with the capital, opening a small shop on this very spot. Sitting here, watching towards the hills, he had often dreamt how he would put up a thatched roof here, spread a gunny sack out on the ground, and display on it fried nuts, coloured sweets, and green coconut for the thirsty and famished wayfarers on the highway, which was sometimes very busy. The animals were not prizes ones for a cattel show, but he had spent his occasional savings to provide them some fancy diet now and then, and they did not look too bad. While he was reflecting thus, the red man shook his hand and left on his palm one hundred rupees in tens now, suddenly realizing that this was what the old man was asking. "It is all for you or you may share it if you have a partner."

The old man pointed at the station wagon and asked. "Are you carrying them off in that?"

"Yes, of course," said the other, understanding the transportation part of it.

The old man said, "This will be their first ride in a motor car. Carry them off after I get out of sight, otherwise they will never follow you, but only me even if I am travelling on the path to Yama Loka." He laughed at his own joke, brought his palms together in a salute, turned around and went off, and was soon out of sight beyond a clump of thicket.

The red man looked at the goats grazing peacefully. Perched on the pedestal of the horse, as the westerly sun touched off the ancient faded colours of the statue with a fresh splendour. he ruminated, "He must be gone to fetch some help, I suppose." and settled down to wait. When a truck came downhill, he stopped it and got the help of a couple of men to detach the horse from its pedestal and place it in his station wagon. He gave them five rupees each, and for a further payment they siphoned off gas from the truck, and helped him to start his engine.

Muni hurried homeward with the cash securely tucked away at his waist in his dhoti. He shut the street door and stole up softly to his wife as she squatted before the lit oven wondering if by a miracle food would drop from the sky. Muni displayed his fortune for the day. She snatched the notes from him, counted them by the glow of the fire, and cried, "One hundred rupees! How did you come by it? Have you been stealing?"

"I have sold our goats to a red-faced man. He was absolutely crazy to have them, gave me all this money and carried them off in his motor car!"

Hardly had these words left his lips when they heard bleating outside. She opened the door and saw the two goats at her door. "Here they are!" she said. "What's the meaning of all this?"

He muttered a great curse and seized one of the goats by its ears and shouted, "Where is that man? Don't you know you are his? Why did you come back?" The goat only wriggled in his grip. He asked the same question of the other, too. The goat shook itself off. His wife glared at him and declared, "If you have thieved, the police will come tonight and break your bones. Don't involve me. I will go away to my parents. ..."

□

7. SELVI

(R. K. Narayan)

At the end of every concert, she was mobbed by autograph hunters. They would hem in and not allow her to leave the dais. At that moment Mohan, slowly progressing towards the exit, would turn round and call her across the hall, 'Selvi, hurry up. You want to miss the train?'

'Still a lot of time,' she could have said, but she was not in the habit of contradicting him; for Mohan this was a golden chance not to be missed, to order her in public and demonstrate his authority. He would then turn to a group of admirers, waiting to escort him and Selvi, particularly Selvi, to the car, and remark in apparent jest, 'Left to herself, she'll sit there and fill all the autograph books in the world till doomsday, she has no sense of time.'

The public viewed her as a rare ethereal entity; but he alone knew her private face. 'Not bad-looking,' he commented within himself when he first saw her, 'but needs touching up.' Her eye-brows, which flourished wildly were trimmed and arched. For her complexion, by no means fair, but just on the border line, he discovered the correct skin cream and talcum which imparted to her brow and cheeks a shade confounding classification. Mohan did not want anyone to suspect that he encouraged the use of cosmetics. He had been a follower of Mahatma Gandhi and spent several years in prison, wore only cloth spun by hand, and shunned all luxury; there could be no question of his seeking modern, artificial aids to enhance the personality of his wife. But he had discovered at some stage, certain subtle cosmetics through a contact in Singapore, an adoring fan of Selvi's who felt only too honoured to be asked to supply them regularly, and to keep it a secret.

When Selvi came on the stage, she looked radiant rather than dark, brown, or fair, and it left the public guessing and debating whenever the question came up, as to what colour her skin was. There was a tremendous amount of speculation on all aspects of her life and person wherever her admirers gathered, especially at a place like The Boardless, where much town-talk was exchanged over coffee at the tables reserved to the habitue. Varma, the proprietor, himself loved to overhear such conversation from his pedestal at the cash counter, especially when the subject was Selvi. He was one of her worshippers but from a distance, often feeling, 'Goddess Lakshmi has favoured me; I have nothing more to pray for in the line of wealth or prosperity, but I crave for the favour of the other Goddess, that is Saraswathi, who is in our midst today as Selvi the divine singer; if only she will condescend to accept a cup of coffee or sweet to from my hand, how grand it would be! But alas, whenever I carry gift for her, he takes it and turns me back from the porch with a formal word of thanks.'

Varma was only one among the thousands who had a longing to meet Selvi. But she was kept in a fortress of invisible walls. It was as if she was fated to spend her life either in solitary confinement or fettered to her gaoler in company. She was never left alone even for a moment with anyone. She had been wedded to Mohan for over two decades and had never spoken to anyone except in his presence.

Visitors kept coming all day long for a *darshan* of Selvi but few ever reached her presence. Some were received on the ground floor, some were received on the lawns, some were encouraged to go up the staircase—but none could get a glimpse of her—but only of Mohan's secretary or the secretary's secretary. Select personalities, however, were received ceremoniously in the main hall upstairs and seated on sofas. Ordinary visitors would not be offered seats, but they could occupy any bench or chair found scattered here and there and wait as long as they pleased—and go back wherever they came from.

Their home was a huge building of East India Company days displaying arches, columns and gables, once the residence of Sir Frederick Lawley, (whose statue stood at the town-square), who had kept a retinue of forty servants to sweep and dust the six over-sized halls built on two floors, with tall doors and Gothic windows, and Venetian shutters; and set on several acres of ground, five miles away from the city on the road to Mempi Hills. The place was wooded with enormous trees, particularly imported was an Elm (or Oak or Beech, no one could say) at the gate, planted by Sir F. Lawley, who had brought the seedling from England, said to be the only of its kind in India. No one would tenant the house since Sir Frederick's spirit was said to hover about the place, and many weird tales were current in Malgudi at that time. The building had been abandoned since 1947, when Britain quit India. Mohan who at some point made a bid for it, said, 'Let me try. Gandhiji's non-violence rid the country of the British rule. I was a humble disciple of Mahatmaji and I should be able to rid the place of at least a British ghost by the same technique!' He found money to buy the house when Selvi received a fee for lending her voice to a film star, who could just move her lips to synchronise with Selvi's singing and attained thus much glory for her performance in a film. But thereafter Mohan definitely shut out all film offers. 'I'll establish Selvi as a unique phenomenon on her own, not as a voice for some fat cosmetic-dummy.'

Bit by bit, by assiduous publicity and word of mouth recommendation, winning the favour of every journalist and music critic available he had built up her image, in its present stature. Hard work it was over the years. At the end when it bore fruit, her name acquired a unique charm, her photograph began to appear in one publication or another every week. She was in demand everywhere. Mohan's office was besieged by the organisers of musical events from all over the country. 'Leave your proposal with my secretary, and we will inform you after finalising our calendar for the quarter,' he would tell one. To another, he would say, 'My schedule is tight till 1982, if there is any cancellation we'll see what can be done. Remind me in October of 1981, I'll give you a final answer.' He rejected several offers for no other reason than to preserve a rarity value for Selvi. When Mohan accepted an engagement, the applicant, (more a supplicant), felt grateful, notwithstanding the exorbitant fee, half to be paid immediately in cash without a receipt. He varied his tactics occasionally. He would specify that all the earnings of a certain concert should go to some fashionable social service organization carrying well-known names on its list of patrons. He would accept no remuneration for the performance itself, but ask for expenses in cash, which would approximate to his normal fee. He was a financial expert who knew how to conjure up money, and at the same time keep Income Tax at arm's length. Pacing his lawns and corridors restlessly, his mind was always busy, planning how to organise and manoeuvre men and money. Suddenly he would pause, summon his stenographer and dictate or pick up the phone and talk at length into it.

In addition to the actual professional matters, he kept an eye on public relations too. He attended select exclusive parties, invited eminent men and women to dinner at Lawley Terrace. Among the guests would often be found a sprinkling of international figures too. On his walls hung group photographs of himself and Selvi in the company of the strangest assortment of personalities — Tito, Bulganin, Yehudi Menuhin, John Kennedy, the Nehru family, the Pope, Charlie Chaplin, Yogis and sportsmen and political figures — taken under various circumstances and settings.

At The Boardless there was constant speculation about Selvi's early life. Varma heard at the gossip table that Selvi had been brought up by her mother in a back row of Vinayak Mudali Street, in a small house with tiles falling off, with not enough cash at home to put the tiles back on the roof and had learnt music from her, practising with her brother and sister accompanying her on their instruments.

At this time Mohan had a photo studio on Market Road, Once Selvi's mother brought the girl to be photographed for a school magazine after she had won the first prize in a music competition.

Thereafter Mohan visited them casually now and then as a sort of well-wisher of the family sat in the single chair their home provided, drank coffee, and generally behaved as a benign god to that family by his advice and guidance. Sometimes he would request Selvi to sing, and then dramatically leave the chair and sit down on the floor cross-legged with his eyes shut, in an attitude of total absorption in her melody, to indicate that in the presence of such an inspired artist it would be blasphemous to sit high in a chair.

Day after day, he performed little services to the family, and then gradually took over the management of their affairs. At The Boardless, no one could relate with certainty at what point exactly he began to refer to Selvi as his wife or where, when, or how, they were married. No one would dare investigate it too closely now.

Mohan had lost no time in investing the money, earned from the film in buying Lawley Terrace. After freshening up its walls with lime wash and paints, on an auspicious day he engaged, Gaffur's taxi and took Selvi and the family to the Terrace.

While her mother, brother and sister, looked excited at the dimension of the house as they passed through the six halls, looked up at the high ceiling and clicked their tongues, Selvi herself showed no reaction. She went through the house as if through the corridors of a museum. Mohan was a little disappointed and asked, 'How do you like this place?' At that all she could say in answer was, 'It looks big.' At the end of the guided tour he launched on a description and history (avoiding the hauntings) of the house. She listened without any show of interest. Her mind seemed to be elsewhere. They were all seated on the gigantic settees of the Company days, which had come with the property, and were left behind because they could not be moved. She didn't seem to notice even the immensity of the furniture on which she was seated. As a matter of fact, as he came to realize later, in the course of their hundreds of concert tours, she was habitually oblivious of her surroundings. In any setting—mansions or five star hotels with luxurious guest rooms and attendants; or a small town or village home with no special facilities or privacy—she looked equally indifferent or contented; washed, dressed, and was ready for the concert at the appointed time in the evening. Most days she never knew or questioned where she was to sing or what fee they were getting. Whenever he said, 'Pack and get ready,' she filled a trunk with her clothes, toiletry and tonic pills and was ready, not even questioning where they were going. She sat in a reserved seat in the train when she was asked to do so, and was ready to leave when Mohan warned her they would have to get off at the next stop. She was undemanding, unenquiring, uncomplaining. She seemed to exist without noticing anything or anyone, rapt in some secret melody or thoughts of her own.

In the course of a quarter century, she had become a national figure; travelled widely in and out of the country. They named her the Goddess of Melody. When her name was announced, the hall, any hall filled up to its capacity and people fought for seats. When she appeared on the dais, her audience was thrilled as if vouchsafed a vision, and she was accorded a thundering ovation. When she settled down, gently cleared her throat, and hummed softly to assist the accompanists tune their instruments, a silence fell among the audience. Her voice possessed a versatility and reach, which never failed to transport her audience. Her appeal was alike to the common unsophisticated listener as to pandits, theorists, and musicologists. Even those who didn't care for any sort of music liked to be seen in her concerts for prestige's sake.

During a concert wherever it might be, Madras, Delhi, London, New York or Singapore, Mohan occupied as a rule the central seat in the first row of the auditorium and riveted his gaze on the singer, leaving people to wonder whether he was lost in her spell or whether he was inspiring her by thought-transference. Though his eyes were on her, his mind would be busy doing complicated arithmetic with reference to monetary problems and he would also watch unobtrusively for any tape-recorder that might, be smuggled into the hall (he never permitted recording), and note slyly the reactions of VIPs flanking him.

He planned every concert in detail. He would sit up in the afternoon with Selvi and suggest gently but firmly, 'Wouldn't you like to start with the *Kalyani Varnam*—the minor one?' And she would say, 'yes', never having been able to utter any other word in her life. He would continue, 'The second item had better be *Thyagaraja's* composition in *Begada,* it'll be good to have a contrasting *Raga,'* and then his list would go on to fill up about four hours. 'Don't bother to elaborate any *Pallavi* for this audience, but work out briefly a little detail in the *Todi* composition. Afterwards you may add any item you like, light *Bhajans, Javalis,* or folk songs,' offering her a freedom which was worthless since the programme as devised would be tight-fitting for the duration of the concerts, which according to his rule, should never exceed four hours. 'But for my planning and guidance, she'd make a mess, which no one realises,' he often reflected.

Everyone curried Mohan's favour and goodwill in the hope that it'd lead him to the proximity of the star. Mohan did encourage a particular class to call on him and received them at the Central Hall of Lawley Terrace; he would call aloud to Selvi when such a person arrived. 'Here is so and so, come!' It could be no ordinary name—only a minister or an IG of Police or the Managing Director of a textile mill or a newspaper editor, who in his turn would always be eager to do some favour to Mohan hoping thereby to be recognised eventually by

Selvi as a special friend of the family. Selvi would come out of her chamber ten minutes after being summoned, and act her part with precision: a wonderful smile, and *namaste* with her palms gently pressed together, which sent a thrill down the spine of the distinguished visitor, who would generally refer to her last concert and confess how deeply moving it had been and how a particular raga kept ringing in his ears all that evening, long after the performance. Selvi had appropriate lines in reply to such praise, 'Of course, I feel honoured that my little effort has pleased a person of your calibre,' while Mohan would interpose with a joke or a personal remark. He didn't want any visitor, however important, to hold her attention, but would draw it to himself at the right moment. At the end Mohan would feel gratified that his tutored lines, gestures, and expressions were perfectly delivered by Selvi. He would congratulate himself on shaping her up so successfully into a celebrity. 'But for my effort, she'd still be another version of her mother and brother, typical Vinayak Mudali Street products and nothing beyond that. I am glad I've been able to train her so well.' In order that she might quickly get out of the contamination of Vinayak Mudali Street, he gently, unobtrusively, began to isolate her from her mother, brother and sister. As time went on, she saw less and less of them. At the beginning a car would be sent to fetch them, once a week. As Selvi's public engagements increased, her mother and others were gradually allowed to fade out of her life. Selvi tried once or twice to speak to Mohan about her mother, but he looked annoyed and said, 'They must be all right. I'll arrange to get them—but where is the time for it? When we are able to spend at least three days at home, we will get them here.' Such a break was rare—generally they came home by train or car and left again within twenty-four hours.

On occasions when they did have the time and if she timidly mentioned her mother, he would almost snap, 'I know, I know, I'll send Mani to Vinayak Street—but some other time. We have asked the Governor to lunch tomorrow and they will expect you to sing, informally of course, for just thirty minutes.' The day after that?' Selvi would put in hesitantly, and he would ignore her and move off to make to telephone call. Selvi understood, and resigned herself to it, and never again mentioned her mother. 'If my own mother can't see me!' she thought again and again in secret anguish, having none to whom she could speak out her feelings.

Mohan, noticing that she didn't bother him about her mother any more, felt happy that she had got over the obsession. 'That's the right way. Only a baby would bother about its mother.' He congratulated himself again on the way he was handling her.

Months and years passed thus, Selvi did not keep any reckoning of it, but went through her career like an automation, switching on and off her music as ordered.

They were in Calcutta for a series of concerts, when news of her mother's death reached her. When she heard it, she refused to come out of her room in the hotel and wanted all her engagements cancelled. Mohan, who went into her room to coax her, swiftly withdrew when he noticed her tear-drenched face and dishevelled hair. All through the train journey back, she kept looking out of the window and never spoke a word, although Mohan did his best to engage her in talk. He was puzzled by her mood. Although she was generally not talkative, she would at least listen to whatever was said to her and intersperse with an occasional monosyllabic comment. Now for a stretch of thirty-six hours journey she never spoke a word nor looked in his direction. When they reached home, he immediately arranged to take her down to Vinayak Mudali Street and accompanied her himself to honour the dead officially, feeling certain that his gesture would be appreciated by Selvi. Both the big car and Mohan in his whitest handspun clothes seemed ill-fitting in those surroundings. His car blocked half the street in which Selvi's mother had lived. Her sister, who had married and had children in Singapore, could not arrive, her brother's whereabouts were unknown. A neighbour dropped in to explain the circumstances of the old lady's death and how they had to take charge of the body and so forth. Mohan tried to cut short his narration and send him away since it was unusual to let a nondescript to go along and talk to Selvi directly. But she said to Mohan, 'You may go back to the Terrace if you like, I'm staying here.' Mohan had not expected her to talk to him in that manner. He felt confused and muttered, 'By all means ... I'll send back the car ...... When do you want it?'

'Never ... I'm staying here as I did before ...'

'How can you? In this street!' She ignored his objection and said, 'My mother was my Guru, here she taught me music, lived and died .... I'll also live and die here; what was good for her is good for me too.'

He had never known her to be so truculent or voluble. She had been for years so mild and complaisant that he never thought she could act or speak beyond what she was taught. He lingered, waited for a while hoping for a change of her mood. Meanwhile the neighbour was going on with his narration, omitting no detail of the old lady's last moments and the problems that arose in connection with the performance of the final obsequies. 'I did not know where to reach you, but finally we carried her across the river and lit the pyre with my own hands and dissolved the ashes in the Sarayu. After all I've known her as a boy, and you remember how I used to call her 'Auntie' and sit up and listen when you were practising ... Oh! not these days of course, I can't afford to buy a ticket or get anywhere near the hall where you sing.'

Mohan watched in consternation. He had never known her to go beyond the script written by him. She had never spoken to anyone or stayed in a company after receiving his signal to terminate the interview and withdraw. Today it didn't work. She ignored his signal, and the man from Vinayak neighbourhood went on in a frenzy of re-living the funeral; he felt triumphant to have been of help on a unique occasion.

After waiting impatiently, Mohan rose to go. 'Anything you want to be sent down?' 'Nothing,' she replied. He saw that she had worn an old sari, and had no make-up or jewellery, having left it all behind at the Terrace.

'You mean to say, you'll need nothing?'

'I need nothing ...'

'How will you manage?' She didn't answer. He asked weakly. 'You have the concert series at Bhopal, shall I tell them to change the date?' First time he was consulting her on such problems.

'Do what you like,' she simply said.

'What do you mean by it?' No answer.

He stepped out and drove away; the car had attracted a crowd, which now turned its attention to Selvi. They came forward to stare at her—a rare luxury for most, the citadel having been impregnable all these years, she had been only a hearsay and a myth to most people Someone said, 'Why did you not come to your mother's help? She was asking for you!' Selvi broke down and was convulsed with sobs.

Three days later Mohan came again to announce: 'On the 30th you have to receive an Honorary Degree at the Delhi University ...' She just shook her head negatively. 'The Prime Minister will be presiding over the function.'

When pressed, she just said, 'Please leave me out of all this, leave me alone, I want to be alone hereafter. I can't bear the sight of anyone...'

'Just this one engagement. Do what you like after that. Otherwise it will be most compromising. Only one day at Delhi, we will get back immediately—also you signed the gramophone contract for recording next month ...' She didn't reply. Her look suggested that it was not her concern. 'You'll be landing me in trouble, at least, the present commitments ...' It was difficult to carry on negotiations with a crowd watching and following every word of their talk. He wished he could have some privacy with her, but this was a one-roomed house, where everybody came and stood about or sat down anywhere. If he could get her alone, he would either coax her or wring her neck. He felt helpless and desperate, and suddenly turned round and left. But he came again a week later. But it proved no better. She neither welcomed him nor asked him to leave. He suggested to her to come up to the car, this time he had brought his small car. She declined his invitation. 'After all that woman was old enough to die,' he reflected. 'This fool is ruining her life ...' He allowed four more weeks for the mourning period and visited her again, but found a big gathering in her house overflowing into the street. She sat at the back of the little hall, holding up her *thambura* and was singing to the audience as if it were an auditorium. A violinist and a drummer had volunteered to play the accompaniments. 'She is frittering away her art,' he thought. She said, 'Come, sit down.' He sat in a corner, listened for a while and slipped away unobtrusively. Again and again, he visited her and found at all hours of the day, people around her, waiting for her music. News about her free music sessions spread. People thronged there in cars, bicycles and on foot. Varma of The Boardless brought a gift box of sweets wrapped in gilt paper, and handed it to Selvi silently and went away, having realized his ambition to approach his Goddess with an offering. Selvi never spoke unnecessarily. She remained brooding and withdrawn all day, not noticing or minding anyone coming in or going out.

Mohan thought he might be able to find her alone at least at night. At eleven o'clock one night he left his car in Market Road and walked to Vinayak Mudali Street. He called in softly through the door of Selvi's house, 'My dear, it's me, I've to talk to you urgently. Please open the door, please,' appealing desperately through the darkened house. Selvi opened a window shutter, just a crack and said firmly, 'go away, it's not proper to come here at this hour. ...' Mohan turned back with a lump in his throat, swearing half-aloud, 'Ungrateful wretch... .

□

8. 'HEAR ME SANJAYA...'

(Shashi Deshpande)

Shall we sit down here, Sanjay? Just for a while? I know you are anxious about your king, I know you want to get back to him, but I need to rest. Not for long, just for a while. And shall I say something to you, Sanjay? There is no need to be anxious about the king any more. Have you not seen how different he seems ever since Gandhari uncovered her eyes? He seems at peace with himself, as if an ancient wrong has been righted. She should have done it long back. What use was it blinding herself? Oh, these futile vows! I sometimes think they're just a cover for the wilfulness of self-willed people. Look at Bhishma! Do you remember those two queens, our mothers-in-law, Gandhari's and mine... no, how can you? I forget sometimes how young you are. You seem to have been with us always. Why, even I can scarcely remember how they looked. They so rarely spoke, except to each other and that in whispers, and moved about so little and so silently it was hard to remember they were there. But later, when I went back to the palace, they began to haunt me. As if the walls had absorbed their whispers, I could feel them about me. And it was then that I learnt their story—and of the third sister no one ever spoke of, of how and why she died.

But why am I talking of those poor, long-dead women? Oh yes, vows, that's right, I was speaking of vows. You known Sanjaya, sometimes I think—if only Bhishma had given up his vow, if he had children of his own, then perhaps these three sisters would have lived normal happy lives—who knows?

Let it go, I know I shouldn't think this way of someone we revered so much. But what can you do to the mind, Sanjay? I can see it makes you uneasy too to hear me speak this way. Or, are you impatient? Don't be in a hurry, Sanjaya, let us leave the king and my sister to themselves for a while. They will have much to talk. You don't seem pleased? Are you sorry, does it hurt you to let her become his eyes after you have played that role for so long? I know how you feel. I felt that way too, when my sons let go of my hand and began to walk, to run. But never mind, Sanjaya, he will still need your eyes. The world you gave him is the world he is familiar with. I wonder, yes I really wonder, if he can be comfortable with Gandhari's world. At our age we don't like change. You are smiling. I know what you think. We have changed our lives ourselves by coming here away from the palace—that's what you're thinking of, aren't you? But this is not change, my son. We are walking the same road we have done all these years. We have only gone on ahead, much further ahead, that's all.

No, Sanjaya, I don't think I want to sit here after all; let us go somewhere else. I don't like to be so close to the river. The sound of the river makes me uneasy, it fills me with strange thoughts. Shall we walk on? Does it tire you to listen to my talk? I don't know why I am speaking so much today. But, may be it is restful for you to listen instead of to talk. Do you know I used to listen to you sometimes when you described the war to the king? My ears thirsted for news then, Oh how my heart hungered for good news. But I wanted the truth—that was why I used to listen to your account. Sanjaya will speak the truth, I used to think, he will not exaggerate. But you did bend the truth—yes, a little—sometimes, didn't you? Your face told me when you did that. The king could not see it and so he never guessed. But I knew. No, no, don't feel ashamed, Sanjaya, we all do it, we all did it, specially during the war ... .

Why am I speaking of the war? We never speak of it, have you noticed? Not a word, no, neither about the living nor about the dead. It's as if it had never happened. But sometimes, at night, I hear the king moaning, I hear him muttering the names of his sons. Gandhari hears him too, I know she is awake though she does not stir. And in the morning when we wake up, we wipe out the knowledge from our minds. Wholly. Nothing happened. Nothing. We are here, three old people and one young man—that's all. Why are you smiling? Because I called you young? But to me you are young. I always think of you as that splendid young man I saw in charge of the king's chariot. You seemed then like Surya's charioteer. Shining and radiant. Yes, yes, I mean it, that was how you looked. Truly.

But that's all over. Tell me, Sanjaya, do you have regrets about having left all that behind? Tell me, honestly, are you happy here? No, no, I think I shouldn't ask you this question. I know the answer. Mother, Yudhishthira said to me, I can't bear to think of the three of you living here like this. Like what? He thinks we are suffering. But we are not. We are free. You feel it too, don't you? There's something here that wipes away everything that is not true, not necessary. And even Gandhari—now she knows what I meant when I said my children needed no pity because they were in the forest. She thought me proud. Proud! Perhaps I am a proud woman, but it's true that I never felt sorry for my children when they were in the forest—away from walls, from servants, spies and scheming sycophants. I knew that freedom too when my children and I wandered in the forests. There was danger, sometimes there was fear, but they were young and they laughed and played and enjoyed the adventure. There was an earlier time too, wasn't there, before the children were born, when I lived in the forest? Yes, that was with my husband and Madri—that was different, very different.

Why do I suddenly remember them? I have not thought of them for a long time. For years, for ages. They seem to be people I knew in some past life, not part of this one at all. And yet there was a time when I used to brood over them, every minute of the day. Do you know how unfair life is to a woman who does not have beauty, Sanjaya? The day they brought Madri home I knew I was not beautiful. Until then I had not known it, perhaps I had not thought about it all. But after that, every day, every moment of every day .... .

No, I won't think of it. It was so long ago and what profit is there in reviving old bitterness? But I can still remember how threatened I felt by her two sons. It seems strange now, doesn't it? Those two, her sons? They are more my sons than my own. Take my sons, look after them, she said. And I was angry. She's escaping, I thought, she's taking away all the glory, leaving the struggle, the drudgery for me. But she was right to go. He needed her more, even in that other world he would have pined for her. I remember sometimes I used to listen to them talking; he had so many pet names for her, so many endearments. For me, there was only one name. You look away. Do you feel awkward listening to me talking of these things? I won't go on. And why should I burn up thinking of all that now. Sometimes I think when they died I died too and a new woman was born. I had to become, yes, a charioteer. I know how you feel, Sanjaya, I know how it is when you drive a chariot, the impatience, the pride, the confidence, the feeling of being in control, the fear of losing it .... .

When Draupadi came into our home I tried to tell her about it, I thought she could take over my burdens. But she was never one to listen. She was so impatient, oh, so impetuous. I sometimes think they do girls a great wrong when they pamper them and make much of them as children; they make them think they matter. Draupadi was too much petted, too much indulged by her father and brother. Oh, I don't blame them; she must have been such a lively, a sparkling child. But it does not help, no it never does. Only her mother, and it was she who told me this once, only her mother kept warning her—don't think you can always get what you want. She must have had a 'why' even for that. Poor girl. Girl! What am I thinking of? She is a woman, a woman who has no more questions, not since she knew her sons were dead. No tears too now. She was tearless, dry-eyed when she bid me farewell But ... but ... how strange, it comes back to me only now, after she took leave of Gandhari, her cheeks were wet. Gandhari's too. They clung to each other, yes, I can remember that. I know what it is: when they look at me they think—what does she know of sorrow, she, who has lost no son? They forget, they all forget ... .

Or do you think, Sanjaya, the truth is that Draupadi has not forgiven me? You seem amazed. Don't you know I have wronged her? Yes, I have. I used to remember it, I used to think of it each time I looked at her. She entered the hut that day with joy, such joy, Sanjaya, I can never forget her face as she looked up at Arjuna. But I looked at the faces of my other sons and for their sakes took the joy away from hers. I could see Yudhishthira's face light up when I told him what they should do, I saw Bhima's joy. I did not look at her then, but later, when I did, it was as if the light in her had been dimmed. Yes, I did her a great wrong. She should have been only Arjuna's wife. She would have looked up to Yudhishthira like a father and Nakul and Sahadeva, they would have been her friends; why, they were like friends, the three of them.

But what about Bhima then? No, I did what I had to do. I had no choice, I tried to tell myself at times, but that is not true. There is always a choice. And yet I must have been very hard to have made the choice I did that day. But I am a hard woman, Sanjaya, a very hard woman. If I had not been hard would I have survived?

You know, Sanjaya, I think it was good I was brought up the way I was—I was never pampered and indulged. But who would have pampered me anyway? My father gave me away—how easily he gave me away. As if I was a bit of property. Don't you think it queer, Sanjaya? And I can't even remember if it made me angry. But I remember I was frightened. I thought my father gave me away to his friend because he was displeased with me. And I thought—what if I displease this man too? Will he give me away to someone else? And so I did everything I could to please him, I tried so hard never to displease him.

But how I hated my new name—Kunti! I never realized it was I they wanted when someone called out that name. Now, if someone called me Pritha I would not know who it was. But there was someone who called me Pritha—yes, even after I became Kunti, there was someone who called me that. Who was it? This is one of the burdens of being old. Some things come back so easily and others ... Who was it who called me by my name? You are smiling, you are wondering why it should matter. I don't know, but it seems terrible to misplace a memory. They are all we have at our age. Who was it? Pritha, Pritha I can hear someone saying and crying. It was by a river, I can remember that ... .

Yes, it comes back. Nothing is so long ago, is it, Sanjaya? The consequences of an act go on and on. It was my nurse who always called me Pritha. But that day, by the river, I told her—I am Kunti now, call me by no other name. I sent her away, I remember. I wanted to be alone. But even when she left me and went away there was no silence. I could still hear the cries of the child, cries that drowned out the sounds of the river. I kept hearing them, however far I went from the river, I could still hear them. It was only that day, when I went to meet him, yes, again by the river, a grown man now and he turned round and faced me, his face cold and distant—it was only after that I stopped hearing the cries, as if the child had died at last. There were so many things I could have said to him—I was too young then, I could have said, I was only a child, I did not understand anything, I only did what they told me to do. But what was the use? He would not have heard me. It was my nurse who had put a bit of armour by him. Let them know he is a Kshatriya, she had said. When I met him after all those years, it was as if he was still wearing that armour. Nothing I said would have penetrated. My son, I called him, but he never called me Mother, not once. Perhaps he was more honest. But he thought too much of his birth. That armour—it never did him any good.

I have no sons, my husband used to cry. He was frightened of going into the darkness like his father had. It was I who had the courage to light that darkness; Madri dared only when she saw my sons. Yes, we gave him sons, Madri and I, five splendid sons. The sons of Pandu, they are called. And I could never claim my own son. It makes me want to laugh sometimes. I never laughed much when I was young. I used to wonder when I heard Madri laughing, beautiful, easy laughter. Perhaps it's easy to laugh when you are loved. Is that why Krishna could laugh so much, so easily? He could make others laugh too, couldn't he, Sanjaya? I remember how angry Draupadi was when she knew about Subhadra. Krishna soother her and comforted her, though it was he who had brought Arjuna and Subhadra together. And he made Draupadi laugh finally, the rogue. Why Sanjaya, you are frowning, you seem, displeased. Is it because I called Krishna a rogue? I know how you revere him, but I love him like my own. He is my brother's son. I knew him so well. Did I? don't know. But I remember he made Draupadi laugh. She was still angry with Subhadra though, for long she nursed her anger. Yet when Abhimanyu died, she was inconsolable.

Dead ... is he really dead. Sanjaya? Did it all really happen and are they all dead, all our sons? Are they all really dead? Or was it just one of those terrible dreams we are happy to wake out of? No, it's true, it happened. Like Gandhari we have opened our eyes too late. What mistakes we make Sanjaya, what terrible mistakes. Is that why we don't speak of the war? Because we are afraid we will ask ourselves Why? What was it all for? I remember the few feeble cries that greeted my sons when it was all over—victors they called them. Victors? It's the dead who are the victors. They know it too now. Yudhishthira walks about like a puppet, Arjuna's eyes are empty, and even Bhima ... .

You know, Sanjaya, seeing the animals here, I have begun thinking that we are wrong, we are foolish, in clinging to our roles for so long. Does a grown deer seek its mother? At some time the bond should snap, it should be over. That is natural, that is wiser. No? You don't agree? But then one should not live long enough to see the sight I saw. These tired old men my sons, I thought? It frightened me... .

That is enough. I am a fool to have spoken of these things. We are wiser not to speak of them. And what need is there? It is all over now; we are at peace, Gandhari the king and I. We want nothing any any more, not for ourselves, nor for our children. That is real freedom, is it not? You know it too, don't you? Is that why... .

But we must go back now, Sanjaya. We have been away too long. Come, come Sanjaya, we must go. The king and my sister must be wondering what has happened to us, the king must be impatient. Where is Sanjaya, he must be asking the queen, why did you let him go? Come let us go. Look, the sun is setting. How bright the light is. It's like... . The sun setting? So soon? There is still time for that, isn't there? But what is that then? There—look there. What is it, Sanjay, what is it, why are you hurrying? You know I am too old, I can't walk fast. Look, it is spreading, the brightness... Oh, now I know. It is not the sunset. I know why the birds are suddenly silent. Yes, let us hurry. I have to be with them, with my brother and sister, we need to be together. But not you, Sanjay, not you. You must leave us. You are stubborn, but you will have to obey the king, I know you will. Yes, there they are, waiting for us. How still they are standing! Look at the king, his head held high, his nose sniffing the smoke. He knows, yes, they know it too. And they are smiling. Let us go to them, Sanjaya. Let us hurry. No, not you. I have to go, I must go ... .

□

9. STEEL HAWK

(Bhabani Bhattacharya)

The news came at sunrise, charing the air with echoes, like the beat of a drum. Men sped off from the fields, wiping earth-stained hands on their loincloths. Women shouted for their children as they hurried past, their voices, swift and shrill. And the children danced with joy, clapping each other on the back, yelling:

"It's the flying wonder, you hear? We'll go ariding in the sky!"

"We'll touch the clouds, you hear? We'll squeeze clouds in our fists to make rain!"

For in the large meadow on the western edge of the Indian village stood the flying wonder, the sun beating on its wings, the crowd around swelling every minute.

Bishan, the carter, had yoked his pair of bullocks and was coming along in hot haste. He cajoled the animals, prodded them with a short, thick rod, and once or twice pulled each one by the tail. "Tchuk, tchuk! Run! Do not fall asleep, dear brother!"

There was not an eye flick of time to lose. The flying wonder would be gone any moment. Who would expect such a chance to cross a man's life twice? Those wonders were seen on the skyways often enough—strange passing birds in the far blue; at night time they were pilgrim stars! But then here was one squatting afield, a mere wagon tied to earth! Why was it here? Just to rest for a bit on solid earth? Or could there be some mystery behind it, some hidden purpose?

The wheels of wood thwacked the deep dust of the road. The bullocks raced, their heavy flanks quaking, their heads dizzy with speed. "Tchuk, tchuk! Run hard, gentlemen, run till you lose your breath!"

As the cart was passing the Balcony of knowledge, where the village school-teacher lived, Kamini, the teacher's young wife, hailed from the doorway: "Oxcart, will you take us to the meadow on which the wonder of wonders has descended?"

Red dust clung to her bare feet. One hand held a half-drawn veil, the other clutched the arm of Babla, her six-year old daughter.

"What fare, Ox-cart?" she added, as the vehicle pulled up alongside.

"Why, Mother, I'm going there to fill my own eyes. How can I charge you a fare?"

The cartman's eyes turned, rose to the thatched kitchen roof, his face beaming. "A-ha, what a pumpkin vine you've raised, what tendrils, lit he and strong, what yellow bells of blooms!"

"The first-fruits of that plant will be yours."

The bargain settled, Kamini climbed in at the cart's rear, with her daughter.

The cow-bells jingled and the cart trekked down the pathway to the meadow, skirting a shadowed mango grove, and turned into a lane between fields of paddy, a red tape zigzagging through sweeps of vivid yellow. The tall paddy, with full-kernelled grain, drooped under the weight of the wind.

"Never will *she* set her two eyes on this wonder!" the cartman spoke softly, as if to himself, shaking his close-cropped head with sadness. "What evil fate that gout holds her bones on this day, of all days! The whole village sees the wonder: she alone is denied."

"Who, Ox-cart?"

"Old Grandma, poor soul. Mad about tricky machines, stark mad! Same today as in her long-ago days, when the railroad first came this way."

"Railroad?" said Kamini, in surprise, "The rail-road came this way countless, years ago."

The cartman smiled. "Grandma is countless years old, isn't she? It happened when she was 14 or 15 ..."

"What happened?" cried Kamini. "Tell me, cartman!" her voice pleaded.

"A railway station was built at Choorni, one hour's walk from our Sonamitti."

"Yes, What then?"

"Grandma was 14 or 15. Wed a short time."

"I am listening," said Kamini, for the cartman had paused again.

"Grandma had seen fire-engines roll past, sooty smoke belching out of the squat nostril. Now at last she could see one standing by, big and quiet as an elephant. She could reach out with her hand, feel the iron skin. Grandpapa read her mind and took her to Choorni one day in his cart."

And now Bishan warmed to his story. He neglected his oxen, turned his face towards his listener and let his voice go faster: "Grandpapa took her to Choorni Station one day. They heard the rumble like twenty thunders and the fire-engine came hotfoot, a monster, with coach after coach of metal and wood, all ashine with paint and glass. For full five breaths Grandma was dead still. The train wouldn't wait long, so Grandpapa warned her, and she at once came back to life. She, first of all, bent low to look at the hundred wheels. Then she walked to the engine, its barrel body all oily with the sweat of toil and moil, took one good look at it and also at the man in blue tunic and trouser who drove the monster. She turned back, peering in here, there, everywhere, to see the lights that needed no oil to make them burn, the fans that needed no hand to stir a breeze, and she turned her eyes this way and that, at this and that passenger, woman, child, man ... .

"At last, when the fire-engine gave a long 'coo-oo' and started to move off, 'whoosh-whoosh-whoosh', coach after coach going fast and smooth, as if gliding on glass, Grandma was dead still again.

"It was a good bit of time before she found her tongue. She turned round to Grandpapa and said: "Truly, such a thing exists! To see this I must have earned merit by a hundred and one good deeds!"

"And she closed her eyes and joined her palms to her forehead, saluting the image of majesty. Grandpapa burst out laughing but his eyes must have been wet. Two or three days later, they went again to Choorni Station, and this time they bought tickets and rode on the train. They rode to the next stop. They walked back home."

Bishan paused a moment, returning from his mind-picture of the past, and his voice came huskily: "Old she is, and as crazy still as in her long-ago days."

"The sadness that she will not see the flying wonder!" Kamini shook her head with pity. "Athrill she would have been, as before."

"She bade me rush and see this machine. She will see it afterwards with *my* eyes. She will want to know everything—how it looks, how it smells..."

There was a silence. The cartman prodded his bullocks. "Hey, brothers of an ass, run! Run hard till you lose your breath! Faster, gentlemen, faster!"

The crowd came into view. The cart drew up in a minute. Bishan unyoked the animals.

"Make way for the mother from the Balcony of Knowledge!" he said, pushing his way gently through the assembled people watching with bated breath.

So small! Bishan felt quite disappointed. A mere grasshopper! So different from what one saw on the skypath! A comic figure with two wheels—as though paved streets ran up there in the sky! A hawk with no legs but wheels! And the wings looked much too stiff to fold or even to flap! A tail with fishlike fin! Blades on the snout, good weapons to fight with! In a battle of the air, the pilot could weild the blades to gore the foe in the guts!

Grandma had not missed much, anyhow. Bishan felt relieved and happy. But, then, he mustn't take away her fond belief. "Grandma," he would say, "the air wagon is twice as big as the fire-engine. Its white body bristles all over with guns, porcupine-like. It is a true fighter, Grandma! It has the soldier's smell, and even to look at it is to feel fear."

Grandma, listening intently, would wag her head with satisfaction. "Just what I thought. The Ramayana, our epic of the olden times, pictures the flying chariot that existed then. Bishan, boy, life is a Great Wheel! It spins slowly in the Stream of Time, a finger's width in a hundred years! Things on top get lost to the view with the Wheel's turning, but, as time flows on, they rise again!"

'Grandma must not lose the flying wonder of her fancy,' Bishan said to himself, decisively.

The machine was about to take off. And no one yet had an inkling why it had landed here.

Man and woman and child held their breath as the pilot smilingly waved his hand at them, turned round and stepped up to his seat. Suddenly, the blades on the snout swung into motion with a zoom that grew more and more—at first a splutter of many sounds, then one big beat. As the machine darted and hopped into the air the crowd first gasped, then broke into a clamour. Loud yells of cheering followed the machine as it climbed skywards.

"Ma," cried Babla, straining her eyes against the sun, "what if birds attack the flying wonder? Fifty, twenty birds?"

"Birds have no malice, darling. They have clean thoughts, all except the crows, and crows cannot get so high."

"What if a pack of ruffian crows get so high, Ma?"

"Then the flying wonder will pour out fumes. the crows will drop down, a heap of feather and beak."

The cartman was bemused as he was walking away, slow-footed. No, that Steel Hawk had not fallen short of Grandma's fancy. What had seemed on land a mere grosshopper grew into splendour up there in the sky. All the same...

The bullocks were munching grass. The cartman yoked them back and stood, leaning over the hump of one animal. The Steel Hawk had great speed and went far faster than all winged creatures. All the same, why must speed greedily eat up the farness? Why ask to reach your journey's end in two hours or three?

Pondering, he could not make it out. Was it not more easeful to rattle along on the road? You could speak to the folks (and no folks to speak to on the skypath), stop and pluck a bloom from the fields or a sprig of tasty green gram, and you could do a hundred other things.

Why must speed greedily eat up the farness?

Grandma would know the answer; she was mad about tricky machines, stark mad. Grandma could look at the flying wonder and go ariding it in her fancy, zooming away mightily and shooting from sky to sky like a crazy star. Grandma had *that* sort of mind. She had it when she was young, and she still had it when her hair was without one black strand, all teeth gone, and sadness and pain written on her brow in each of a hundred wrinkles, graven deep.

Bishan twisted his face, feeling a tenderness in him and yet a superiority, a knowingness. Grandma's spirit was catching up with him! She who was of Yesterday was possessed by Today. Then how could one who was of Today be otherwise? Could one belong in one's mind to whatever time one liked? Could one person ever exchange roots with another, exchange the breath in his nostrils?

He lifted his face skywards, his eyes hard with a kind of challenge.

What if *she* could be there, the aged Grandma, riding the Steel Hawk? And Bishan felt his heart swell. Wouldn't she be even more thrilled than when she saw the fire-engine for the first time; or when, two or three days later, she rode in one of the rumbling, rocking coaches?

Truly, such a thing exists! To see this I must have earned merit by a hundred and one good deeds?

And Bishan, shading his eyes with his palm and turning them to the far sky, surrendered himself to his fancy ... There she was, the aged Grandma, with her modern dream, riding the Steel Hawk, soaring atop!

'Ho, pilot brother, take need lest you lose you bearings! Take heed lest you brush against a shooting star or move too close to the sun-god! Take heed lest you be pulled into the dark realm of baleful Saturn! Take heed lest you be doomed to wander forlorn on the skyways, never to return to earth! Take all heed, ho, pilot brother!'

Impatient cow-bells tinkled into his reverie while he leaned against the fat, white flanks of an ox, but his neck remained craned, his mind remote. For the cartman of Sonamitti village had yielded to the impulse of the age and was riding the Steel Hawk with his Grandma, zooming away mightily.

□

10. THE THIEF

(Ruskin Bond)

I was still a thief when I met Arun, and thought I was only fifteen, I was an experienced and fairly successful hand.

Arun was watching the wrestlers when I approached him. He was about twenty, a tall, lean fellow, and he looked kind and simple enough for my purpose. I hadn't had much luck of late, and thought I might be able to get into this young person's confidence. He seemed quite fascinated by the wrestling. Two well-oiled men slide about in the soft mud, grunting and slapping their thighs. When I got Arun into conversation he didn't seem to realise I was a stranger.

'You look like a wrestler yourself,' I said.

'So do you,' he replied, which put me out of my stride for a moment, because at the time I was rather thin and bony and not very impressive physically.

'Yes,' I said. 'I wrestle sometimes.'

'What's your name?'

'Deepak,' I lied.

Deepak was about my fifth name. I had earlier called myself Ranbir, Sudhir, Trilok, and Surinder.

After this preliminary exchange, Arun confined himself to comments on the match, and I didn't have much to say. After a while he walked away from the crowd of spectators. I followed him.

'Hallo,' he said. 'Enjoying youself?'

I gave him my most appealing smile. 'I want to work for you,' I said.

He didn't stop walking. 'And what makes you think I want some one to work for me?'

'Well,' I said, 'I've been wandering about all day, looking for the best person to work for. When I saw you, I knew that no one else had a chance.'

'You flatter me,' he said.

'That's all right.'

'But you can't work for me.'

'Why not?'

'Because I can't pay you.'

I thought that over for a minute. Perhaps I had misjudged my man.

'Can you feed me?' I asked.

'Can you cook?' he countered.

'I can cook,' I lied.

'If you can cook,' he said, 'I'll feed you.'

He took me to his room and told me I could sleep in the verandah. But I was nearly back on the street that night. The meal I cooked must have been pretty awful, because Arun gave it to the neighbour's cat and told me to be off. But I just hung around smiling in my most appealing way; and then he couldn't help laughing. He sat down on the bed and laughed for a full five minutes, and later patted me on the head and said, never mind, he'd teach me to cook in the morning.

Not only did he teach me to cook, but he taught me to write my name and his, and said he would soon teach me to write whole sentences, and add money on paper when you didn't have any in your pocket!

It was quite pleasant working for Arun. I made the tea in the morning and later went out shopping. I would take my time buying the day's supplies and made a profit of about 25 paise a day. I would tell Arun that rice was 56 paise a pound (it generally was), but I would get it as 50 paise a pound. I think he knew I made a little this way, but he didn't mind, he wasn't giving me a regular wage.

I was really grateful to Arun for teaching me to write. I knew that once I could write like an educated man there would be no limit to what I could achieve. It might even be an incentive to be honest.

Arun made money by fits and starts. He would be borrowing one week, lending the next. He would keep worrying about his next cheque but, as soon as it arrived, he would go out and celebrate lavishly.

One evening he came home with a wad of notes, and at night I saw him tuck the bundles under his mattress, at the head of the bed.

I had been working for Arun for nearly a fortnight and, apart from the shopping, hadn't done much to exploit him. I had every opportunity for doing so. I had a key to the front door, which meant I had access to the room whenever Arun was out. He was the most trusting person I had ever met. And that was why I couldn't make up my mind to rob him.

It's easy to rob a greedy man, because he deserves to be robbed; it's easy to rob a rich man, because he can afford to be robbed; but it's difficult to rob a poor man, even one who really doesn't care if he's robbed. A rich man or a greedy man or a careful man wouldn't keep his money under a pillow or mattress, he'd lock it up in a safe place. Arun had put his money where it would be child's play for me to remove it without his knowledge.

It's time I did some real work, I told myself; I'm getting out of practice ... If I don't take the money, he'll only waste it on his friends ... He doesn't even pay me ... .

Arun was asleep. Moonlight came in from the verandah and fell across the bed. I sat up on the floor, my blanket wrapped round me, considering the situation. There was quite a lot of money in that wad, and if I took it I would have to leave town—I might make the 10.30 express to Amritsar ... .

Slipping out of the blanket, I crept on all fours through the door and up to the bed, and peeped at Arun. He was sleeping peacefully with a soft and easy breathing. His face was clear and unlined; even I had more markings on my face, though mine were mostly scars.

My hand took on an identity of its own as it slid around under the mattress, the fingers searching for the notes. They found them, and I drew them out without a crackle.

Arun sighed in his sleep and turned on his side, towards me. My free hand was resting on the bed, and his hair touched my fingers.

I was frightened when his hair touched my fingers, and crawled quickly and quietly out of the room.

When I was in the street, I began to run. I ran down the bazaar road to the station. The shops were all closed, but a few lights came from upper windows. I had the note at my waist, held there by the string of my pyjamas. I felt I had to stop and count the notes though. I knew it might make me late for the train. It was already 10.20 by the clock tower. I slowed down to a walk, and my fingers flicked through the notes. There were about a hundred rupees in fives. A good haul. I could live like a prince for a month or two.

When I reached the station I did not stop at the ticket-office (I had never bought a ticket in my life) but dashed straight on to the platform. The Amritsar Express was just moving out. It was moving slowly enough for me to be able to jump on the foot-board of one of the carriages, but I hesitated for some urgent, unexplainable reason.

I hesitated long enough for the train to leave without me.

When it had gone, and the noise and busy confusion of the platform had subsided, I found myself standing alone on the deserted platform. The knowledge that I had a hundred stolen rupees in my pyjamas only increased my feeling of isolation and loneliness. I had no idea where to spend the night; I had never kept any friends, because sometimes, friends can be one's undoing; I didn't want to make myself conspicuous by staying at a hotel. And the only person I knew really well in town was the person I had robbed!

Leaving the station, I walked slowly through the bazar keeping to dark, deserted alleys. I kept thinking of Arun. He would still be asleep, blissfully unaware of his loss.

I have made a study of men's faces when they have lost something of material value. The greedy man shows panic, the rich man shows anger, the poor man shows fear; but I knew that neither panic nor anger nor fear would show on Arun's face, when he discovered the theft; only a terrible sadness not for the loss of the money but for my having betrayed his trust.

I found myself on the *maidan* and sat down on a bench with my feet tucked up under my haunches. The night was a little cold, and I regretted not having brought Arun's blanket along. A light drizzle added to my discomfort. Soon it was raining heavily. My shirt and pyjamas stuck to my skin and a cold wind brought the rain whipping across my face. I told myself that sleeping on a bench was something, I should have been used to by now, but the verandah had softened me.

I walked back to the bazar and sat down on the step of a closed shop. A few vagrants lay beside me, rolled up tight in thin blankets. The clock showed midnight, I felt for the notes; they were still with me, but had lost their crispness and were damp with rainwater.

Arun's money. In the morning he would probably have given me a rupee to go to the pictures but now I had it all. No more cooking his meals, running to the bazaar, or learning to write whole sentences. Whole sentences ... .

They were something I had forgotten in the excitement of a hundred rupees. Whole sentences, I knew, could one day bring me more than a hundred rupees. It was a simple matter to steal (and sometimes just as simple to be caught) but to be a really big man, a wise and successful man, that was something. I should go back to Arun, I told myself, if only to learn how to write.

Perhaps it was also concern for Arun that drew me back; a sense of sympathy is one of my weaknesses, and through hesitation over a theft I had often been caught. A successful theif must be pitiless. I was fond of Arun. My affection for him, my sense of sympathy, but most of all my desire to write whole sentences, drew me back to the room.

I hurried back to the room extremely nervous, for it is easier to steal something than to return it undetected. If I was caught beside the bed now, with the money in my hand, or with my hand under the mattress there could be only one explanation: that I was actually stealing. If Arun woke up, I would be lost.

I opened the door clumsily, then stood in the doorway in clouded moonlight. Gradually my eyes became accustomed to the darkness of the room. Arun was still asleep. I went on all fours again and crept noiselessly to the head of the bed. My hand came up with the notes. I felt his breath on my fingers. I was fascinated by his tranquil features and easy breathing and remained motionless for a minute. Then my hand explored the mattress, found the edge, slipped under it with the notes.

I awoke late next morning to find that Arun had already made the tea. I found it difficult to face him in the harsh light of day. His hand was stretched out towards me. There was a five-rupee note between his fingers. My heart sank.

'I made some money yesterday,' he said, 'Now you'll get paid regularly.' My spirit rose as rapidly as they had fallen. I congratulated myself on having returned the money.

But when I took the note, I realised that he knew everything. The note was still wet from last night's rain.

'Today I'll teach you to write a little more than your name,' he said.

He knew; but neither his lips nor his eyes said anything about their knowing.

I smiled at Arun in my most appealing way; and the smile came by itself, without my knowing it.

□

11. THE VOICE OF GOD

(Khushwant Singh)

Bhamba Kalan and Bhamba Khurd are two little villages with hardly half a mile between them. As a matter of fact, the littering of mud huts, the tomb of Syed Bulhey Shah and the Mission School almost link Bhamba Kalan and Bhamba Khurd together; hence they are generally referred to as just Bhamba.

The village is mainly inhabited by Sikh peasants, who own all the land around it. The Moslems till the lands of their Sikh masters or ply the lesser trades as potters and weavers. There are some Christians who live in a cluster of huts on the outskirts of the habitations who do the menial work. Then there are the Hindu shopkeepers who sell provisions—oil, soap, salt, spices, cloth, scissors, mirrors and Japanese toys.

Nothing that is important ever happens in Bhamba. Once a year there is a gathering at the tomb of Syed Bulhey Shah when people from the neighbouring villages—Moslems, Hindus and Sikhs alike—come to the fair. Their womenfolk make offerings at the tomb and buy charms to induce their barren wombs to yield. Once a year the Sikhs go to the fair at Amritsar with their long swords carried on their shoulders. Besides these, the only excitement is provided by periodical visits of the police. Someone would break someone else's head in a drunken brawl; someone would abduct somebody's wife or daughter; someone would be indiscreet in distilling illicit liquor. Sometimes no one would do anything and the police would simply come to drink the illicit liquor and eat the eggs and chickens. From the homes of the inhospitable the police would recover arms, liquor or opium, and they would be sent to jail or learn to be hospitable.

Besides these diversions, life in Bhamba has little change. In the morning, while men work in the fields and boys graze cattle, women work at home grinding corn, cooking or spinning, After midday they all relax. The flour mill starts working. It has a diesel oil engine with an exhaust pipe rising above the village roofs. On top of the exhaust pipe the miller has fixed an earthen pot which turns the engine's puffing into shrill blasts. Its monotonous notes are heard for miles around Bhamba. It is the background music to afternoon siestas and lazy gossip.

One spring afternoon the residents of Bhamba were basking in the sunshine in little groups doing nothing. The men sat on their haunches, staring blankly at the mud walls, listening to the music of the mill. The women sat on their string cots gossiping and rubbing clarifed butter into each other's scalps. There was a bumper crop in the offing, and the vast stretch of yellow and green mustard gave the countryside an appearance of peace and prosperity.

All at once the village was astir. Children went running about the alleys shouting excitedly. A motor car ploughed its way through the dusty track towards Bhamba raising clouds of dust behind it. It was a smart brown station wagon with five or six people in it. The car drove up hooting furiously. Children ran behind it or stood on its rear bumper. Village dogs were all around, barking and snapping at the mudguards. The car came to a halt in the village square, and the clouds of dust raised by it rolled up and eveloped it.

When the dust drifted away five men stepped out with handkerchiefs to their noses. In front was the English Deputy Commissioner, Mr. Forsythe—a short stout man in khaki with a sola topee tightly strapped under his chin. He was escorted by two policemen and his chauffeur. With him was Sardar Sahib Ganda Singh, Honorary Magistrate, a big landowner who lived in and owned the neighbouring village, Ganda Singh Wala.

The zaildar and three lambardars of Bhamba stepped out from the crowd of villagers and greeted the Englishman with salams and a chorus of welcome. The Sahib had never been to Bhamba before. What auspicious occasion had brought the defender of the poor, the king of kings, the merciful, to these parts?

The Deputy Commissioner smiled affably and made for the house of the zaildar. Mr. Forsythe sank into a low cane chair while his companion, Ganda Singh, sat next to him on a green one made of steel. The villagers closed round the circle of chairs, still a babel of welcomes.

Forsythe took off his sola topee, uncovering a pink bald head. He mopped his forehead with his handkerchief and with a gesture indicated to the crowd that he wished to speak. There was silence. Forsythe continued to mop his forehead to let the silence sink into the crowd and increase their expectancy. Then he introduced Ganda Singh in eloquent terms.

Ganda Singh did not need an introduction. Everyone in the district knew him. He had helped the Government and had been granted lands, titles and an Honorary Magistracy. He was a well-known patron of thugs. His men robbed with impunity and shared the proceeds with the police. His liquor stills worked in broad daylight and even excise staff were entertained to many varieties of liquor fermented in dung heaps. Ganda Singh's hospitality was lavish. There was food and drink in plenty. For men who mattered. he even provided dusky village maidens—naive and provocatively unwilling.

Ganda Singh was the most hated man in the district, and he knew it. Wherever he went, he was accompanied by two armed men. black leather cartridge belt charged with bullets ran across his chest from the shoulder to the hips, ending in a pouch containing a loaded revolver. Everyone in Bhamba had seen him before. His starched turban had one end proudly plumaged above his head and the other hanging behind the nape of his neck. His eyes were darkened with antimony and his glossy black beard, nearly trimmed and oiled, gave him a lecherous look. He was tall and corpulent. He wore a white shirt which hung just above his knees and a pair of baggy punjabi trousers whose blue silk cord was displayed under the hem of the shirt. On his feet he wore a pair of black pump which squeaked as he walked.

Forsythe paid tributes to Ganda Singh as the pride of the district. He was glad to learn, he said, that the Sardar was proposing to contest the forthcoming elections to the Punjab Legislative Assembly. He had been nominated by the leaders of the Sikh community and had the full approval of the Government.

There were whispers and subdued talk but Forsythe did not attach any importance to them. He dismissed the crowd and then proceeded to talk revenue business with the zaildar and the lambardars.

While Forsythe was busy with one lambardar, Ganda Singh canvassed the others a few yards away with his arms round their shoulders. He told them that the Sahib was very 'merciful to him' and he could get him to do anything the lambardars wanted. One wanted a licence for a gun. Another's name had been sent up to the Deputy Commissioner to be made an assessor in the Court of Sessions. The third one's nephew had been run in under the Excise Act and his case was pending. Could the Deputy Commissioner drop a hint to the Magistrate that the accused was his own man? Ganda Singh made a note of all these in his diary and got the lambardar's promise of 100 per cent poll in his favour. It was a matter of prestige for the Sikh peasantry, he added. More than that, he was of the same sub-caste as they were. As for his rival, the Nationalist candidate, he was not even an agriculturist! He was a lawyer from the city. The Kisan candidate was one of them, but then he had no religion. Besides that, the Government strongly disapproved of him and had frequently put him in jail for reasons of security.

Forsythe and Ganda Singh's party left in the evening. Their visit was like a stone dropped in Bhamba's placid pool whose ripples would take several days to subside. Peace had gone from Bhamba for some time to come.

Next day the residents of Bhamba were again basking in the sunshine listening to the whistling of the grinding machine and talking about Forsythe, when they were disturbed by the shouts of the children and the barking of the dogs. This time the intruder was a large cream-coloured lorry with a loudspeaker fixed on its roof. Along the mudguards on eitherside were fixed stout flag poles on which large-sized flags of the Nationalist party fluttered.

The lorry came to a halt in the village square. Before the dust drifted away and the occupants of the lorry could be made out, the loudspeaker blared out. After a little coughing a voice announced:

'Residents of Bhamba, do you know that elections to the Punjab Assembly are imminent? Do you know your duty in these elections? Vote for Sardar Kartar Singh, Advocate, who is a nominee of the Nationalists!'

There was a pause. Then the voice at the microphone shouted the name of Kartar Singh and a dozen voices yelled back: 'Zindabad!' This was repeated several times in such explosions that dogs put their tails between their legs and slunk away.

Then Kartar Singh stepped out from the front seat. From the rear emerged a dozen young men dressed in Gandhi caps, shirts and dhoties of coarse handspun cloth. They carried bundles of posters.

Kartar Singh had never been to Bhamba before but several villagers knew him. They had engaged him in criminal cases for exorbitant fees. Even these villagers found it difficult to recognize him. They had seen him in European dress with black coat, tie and striped trousers. Now he was dressed in a long shirt, pyjamas and sandals.

Kartar Singh and one of his companions, a fat, dark man dressed like him, made for the zaildar's house, while the other men went about pasting posters in the village. The zaildar's door was shut and he could not be found. The villagers swore that he was with them when the lorry came and had left to make arrangements for the visitors. But the zaildar's little boy came out of his house and informed them that his father had just gone out to answer the call of nature. The villagers smiled and the crowd returned to the lorry. Kartar Singh and his companion clambered on to the roof and the microphone was handed over to them.

Kartar Singh introduced his companion, Seth Sukhtankar. The Seth was a well-known Nationalist leader who had been elected to the Punjab Assembly unopposed. He was also a millionaire, owning a chain of cloth mills. He had made his fortune during the movement to boycott foreign cloth. In the five years of the war the Seth's wealth had gone into astronomical figures. He had no sympathy with the Government, so he bought and sold in the black market with a clear conscience. While people starved and went naked, the Seth bought stacks of wheat and hoarded it. He sold this at fabulous prices. He was passionately anti-British. He wanted all Indians to unite. The main point of his speech was that if 400 million Indians united and spat in a tank, there would be enough spit to drown the entire English population in India. But somehow the facilities for such a mass suicide had never been provided. The Seth was also passionately anti-Socialist. Socialists were traitors. They had caused strikes in his mills at a time when he could have ousted all foreign goods from the market by dumping his own cheaper products. He decried them as foreign agents.

After Sukhtankar, Kartar Singh himself spoke. He knew all about Ganda Singh. No one, he said, should vote for a man who trimmed his beard and drank liquor. He also warned the villagers against the insidious propaganda of the Kisans, who had no religion or morals, and who, besides wanting to share everyone's property, would share everyone's wives.

Seth Sukhtankar's party went as it had come, leaving clouds of dust with the loudspeaker blaring 'Zindabad!' to Kartar Singh's name.

Every day strangers came to Bhamba and made speeches. The private life of Ganda Singh was no longer private. But what of that? retorted Ganda Singh's men. He was a Sikh agriculturist and what agriculturist did not drinks Kartar Singh was only a city lawyer backed by Hindu moneylenders. Didn't Seth Sukhtankar offer money to the lambardars if they proclaimed their intention to vote Nationalist? Where did all the money for lorries, posters and voters come from? Kartar Singh was not too prosperous for a lawyer.

In spite of the slanders against each other, both the candidates agreed that the Kisan should be kept out. But no Kisan had yet come to Bhamba and the villagers awaited with anxiety the arrival of the representative of the godless, immoral traitors.

Then one spring afternoon when, as on any other spring afternoon, the villagers basked in the sunshine doing nothing, the Kisan came. He was not greeted by the village children or the dogs because no one heard him come. He rode up on a mare as white as his turban and the long beard that covered the best part of his chest.

It was Baba Ram Singh. Everyone in Bhamba had heard of him. He had been arrested several times in peasant movements and had spent the best part of his life in jail. All his property had been confiscated and he was homeless—yet all the homes of the countryside were open to him People touched his feet wherever he went and mothers brought their children to be blessed by him. He was popularly known as Babaji, because of his age and piety.

The villagers gathered round Ram Singh, kissing his stirrups and his dusty shoes. What had brought Babaji to Bhamba? He told them that he was contesting the elections to the Legislative Assembly. There was a murmur of applause. Then one villager asked him—

surely the Nationalists could not put up two candidates? Kartar Singh, the lawyer, had told them that he was the Nationalist nominee. The Baba's answer chilled his audience to silence.

'Kisan!'

Kisan? But he was a god-fearing man who had spent his life serving the peasants. Traitor? But the Government had put him in jail for nearly twenty years and robbed him of his property. Immoral? Why, he was like the Guru himself. He did not drink not trim his beard.

Baba Ram Singh did not stay very long. He wanted their votes because he would fight for their liberation from foreigners as well as exploiting landlords. He would fight the police bullies and the corrupt administration. He did not even mention the names of his rival candidates.

No Kisan ever came to Bhamba again. Nor did the Baba himself repeat his visit. He went alone from village to village and in his own peaceful way he blew away the might of Forsythe's Government and the corrupting cash of Sukhtankar like fluffs of thistle-down before a gust of wind.

One day before the polling was to take place, he was arrested on a charge of making a seditious speech.

II

Bhamba like all neighbouring villages went to the polls. Smelly, dirty Sikh peasants tumbled out of Seth Sukhtankar's lorries drunk with Ganda Singh's liquor. But they knew who to vote for. Thousands went in and, being illiterate, named their candidate—and walked back home. The Seth's lorries did not take them back nor did Ganda Singh given them more liquor for sustenance.

The counting was done ten days later in Forsythe's office. A large crowd gathered outside yelling the names of Ganda Singh and Kartar Singh. Baba Ram Singh was not even mentioned. At 11 a.m. the stubby figure of Forsythe appeared on the steps of the office. He was wreathed in smiles as he read out the result.

1. Sardar Ganda Singh, Honorary Magistrate	10,560
2. Sardar Kartar Singh, Advocate	8,340
3. Baba Ram Singh	760

The last mentioned forfeited his deposit.

The people had spoken. The voice of the people is the voice of God.

□

12. SEXY

(Jhumpa Lahiri)

IT WAS A WIFE'S WORST NIGHTMARE. After nine years of marriage, Laxmi told Miranda, her cousin's husband had fallen in love with another woman. He sat next to her on a plane, on a flight from Delhi to Montreal, and instead of flying home to his wife and son, he got off with the woman at Heathrow. He called his wife, and told her he'd had a conversation that had changed his life, and that he needed time to figure things out. Laxmi's cousin had taken to her bed.

"Not that I blame her," Laxmi said. She reached for the Hot Mix she munched throughout the day, which looked to Miranda like dusty orange cereal. "Imagine. An English girl, half his age." Laxmi was only a few years older than Miranda, but she was already married, and kept a photo of herself and her husband, seated on a white stone bench in front of the Taj Mahal, tacked to the inside of her cubicle, which was next to Miranda's. Laxmi had been on the phone for at least an hour, trying to calm her cousin down. No one noticed; they worked for a public radio station, in the fund-raising department and were surrounded by people who spent all day on the phone, soliciting pledges.

"I feel worst for the boy," Laxmi added. "He's been at home for days. My cousin said she can't even take him to school."

"It sounds awful," Miranda said. Normally Laxmi's phone conversations—mainly to her husband, about what to cook for dinner—distracted Miranda as she typed letters, asking members of the radio station to increase their annual pledge in exchange for a tote bag or an umbrella. She could hear Laxmi clearly, her sentences peppered every now and then with an Indian word, through the laminated wall between their desks. But that afternoon Miranda hadn't been listening. She'd been on the phone herself, with Dev, deciding where to meet later that evening.

"Then again, a few days at home won't hurt him." Laxmi ate some more Hot Mix, then put it away in a drawer. "He's something of a genius. He has a Punjabi mother and a Bengali father, and because he learns French and English at school he already speaks four languages. I think he skipped two grades."

Dev was Bengali, too. At first Miranda thought it was a religion. But then he pointed it out to her, a place in India called Bengal, in a map printed in an issue of *The Economist.* He had brought the magazine specially to her apartment, for she did not own an atlas, or any other books with maps in them. He'd pointed to the city where he'd been born, and another city where his father had been born. One of the cities had a box around it, intended to attract the reader's eye. When Miranda asked what the box indicated, Dev rolled up the magazine, and said, "Nothing you'll ever need to worry about," and he tapped her playfully on the head.

Before leaving her apartment he'd tossed the magazine in the garbage, along with the ends of the three cigarettes he always smoked in the course of his visits. But after she watched his car disappear down Commonwealth Avenue, back to his house in the suburbs, where he lived with his wife, Miranda retrieved it, and brushed the ashes off the cover, and rolled it in the opposite direction to get it to lie flat. She got into bed, still rumpled from their lovemaking, and studied the borders of Bengal. There was a bay below and mountains above. The map was connected to an article about something called the Gramin Bank. She turned the page, hoping for a photograph of the city where Dev was born, but all she found were graphs and grids. Still, she stared at them, thinking the whole while about Dev, about how only fifteen minutes ago he'd propped her feet on top of his shoulders, and pressed her knees to her chest, and told her that he couldn't get enough of her.

She'd met him a week ago, at Filene's. She was there on her lunch break, buying discounted pantyhose in the Basement. Afterward she took the escalator to the main part of the store, to the cosmetics department, where soaps and creams were displayed like jewels, and eye shadows and powders shimmered like butterflies pinned behind protective glass. Though Miranda had never bought anything other than a lipstick, she liked walking through the cramped, confined maze, which was familiar to her in a way the rest of Boston still was not. She liked negotiating her way past the women planted at every turn, who sprayed cards with perfume and waved them in the air; sometimes she would find a card days afterward, folded in her coat pocket, and the rich aroma, still faintly preserved, would warm her as she waited on cold mornings for the T.

That day, stopping to smell one of the more pleasing cards, Miranda noticed a man standing at one of the counters. He held a slip of paper covered in a precise, feminine hand. A sales-woman took one look at the paper and began to open drawers. She produced an oblong cake of soap in a black case, a hydrating mask, a vial of cell renewal drops, and two tubes of face cream. The man was tanned, with black hair that was visible on his knuckles. He wore a flamingo pink shirt, a navy blue suit, a camel overcoat with gleaming leather buttons. In order to pay he had taken off pigskin gloves. Crisp bills emerged from a burgundy wallet. He didn't wear a wedding ring.

"What can I get you, honey?" the saleswoman asked Miranda. She looked over the tops of her tortoiseshell glasses, assessing

Miranda's complexion.

Miranda didn't know what she wanted. All she knew was that she didn't want the man to walk away. He seemed to be lingering, waiting, along with the saleswoman, for her to say something. She stared at some bottles, some short, others tall, arranged on all oval tray, like a family posing for a photograph.

"A cream," Miranda said eventually.

"How old are you?"

"Twenty-two."

The saleswoman nodded, opening a frosted bottle. "This may seem a bit heavier than what you're used to, but I'd start now. All your wrinkles are going to form by twenty-five. After that they just start showing."

While the saleswoman dabbed the cream on Miranda's face, the man stood and watched. While Miranda was told the proper way to apply it, in swift upward strokes beginning at the base of her throat, he spun the lipstick carousel. He pressed a pump that dispensed cellulite gel and massaged it into the back of his ungloved hand. He opened a jar, leaned over and drew so close that a drop of cream flecked his nose.

Miranda smiled, but her mouth was obscured by a large brush that the saleswoman was sweeping over her face. "This is blusher Number Two," the woman said, "Gives you some color."

Miranda nodded, glancing at her reflection in one of the angled mirrors that lined the counter. She had silver eyes and skin as pale as paper, and the contrast with her hair, as dark and glossy as an espresso bean, caused people to describe her as striking, if not pretty. She had a narrow, egg-shaped head that rose to a prominent point. Her features, too, were narrow, with nostrils so slim that they appeared to have been pinched with a clothespin. Now her face glowed, rosy at the cheeks, smoky below the brow bone. Her lips glistened.

The man was glancing in a mirror, too, quickly wiping the cream from his nose. Miranda wondered where he was from. She thought he might be Spanish, or Lebanese. When he opened another jar, and said, to no one in particular. "This one smells like pineapple," she detected only the hint of an accent.

"Anything else for you today?" the salewoman asked, accepting Miranda's credit card.

"No thanks."

The woman wrapped the cream in several layers of red tissue. "You'll be very happy with this product." Miranda's hand was unsteady as she signed the receipt. The man hadn't budged.

"I threw in a sample of our new eye gel," the saleswoman added, handing Miranda a small shopping bag. She looked at Miranda's credit card before sliding it across the counter. "Bye-bye, Miranda."

Miranda began walking. At first she sped up. Then, noticing the doors that led to Downtown Crossing, she slowed down.

"Part of your name is Indian," the man said, pacing his steps with hers.

She stopped, as did he, at a circular table piled with sweaters, flanked with pinecones and velvet bows. "Miranda?"

"Mira. I have an aunt named Mira."

His name was Dev. He worked in an investment bank back that way, he said, tilting his head in the direction of South Station. He was the first man with a mustache, Miranda decided, she found handsome.

They walked together toward Park Street station, past the kiosks that sold cheap belts and handbags. A fierce January wind spoiled the part in her hair. As she fished for a token in her coat pocket, her eyes fell to his shopping bag. "And those are for her?"

"Who?"

"Your Aunt Mira."

"They're for my wife." He uttered the words slowly, holding Miranda's gaze. "She's going to India for a few weeks." He rolled his eyes. "She's addicted to this stuff."

Somehow, without the wife there, it didn't seem so wrong. At first Miranda and Dev spent every night together, almost. He explained that he couldn't spend the whole night at her place, because his wife called every day at six in the morning, from India, where it was four in the afternoon. And so he left her apartment at two, three, often as late as four in the morning, driving back to his house in the suburbs. During the day he called her every hour, it seemed, from work, or from his cell phone. Once he learned Miranda's schedule he left her a message each evening at five-thirty, when she was on the T coming back to her apartment, just so, he said, she could hear his voice as soon as she walked through the door. "I'm thinking about you," he'd say on the tape. "I can't wait to see you." He told her he liked spending time in her apartment, with its kitchen counter no wider than a breadbox, and scratchy floors that sloped, and a buzzer in the lobby that always made a slightly embarrassing sound when he pressed it. He said he admired her for moving to Boston, where she knew no one, instead of remaining in Michigan, where she'd grown and gone to college. When Miranda told him it was nothing to admire, that she'd moved to Boston precisely for that reason, he shooks his head. "I know what it's like to be lonely," he said, suddenly serious, and at that moment Miranda felt that he understood her—understood how she felt some nights on the T, after seeing a movie on her own, or going to a bookstore to read magazines, or having drinks with Laxmi, who always had to meet her husband at Alewife station in an hour or two. In less serious moments Dev said he liked that her legs were longer than her torso, something he'd observed the first time she walked across a room naked. "You're the first," he told her, admiring her from the bed. "The first woman I've known with legs this long."

Dev was the first to tell her that. Unlike the boys she dated in college, who were simply taller heavier versions of the ones she dated in high school, Dev was the first always to pay for things, and hold doors open, and reach across a table in a restaurant to kiss her hand. He was the first to bring her a bouquet of flowers so immense she'd had to split it up into all six of her drinking glasses, and the first to whisper her name again and again when they made love. Within days of meeting him, when she was at work, Miranda began to wish that there were a picture of her and Dev tacked to the inside of her cubicle, like the one of Laxmi and her husband in front of the Taj Mahal. She didn't tell Laxmi about Dev. She didn't tell anyone. Part of her wanted to tell Laxmi, if only because Laxmi was Indian, too. But Laxmi was always on the phone with her cousin these days, who was still in bed, whose husband was still in London, and whose son still wasn't going to school. "You must eat something," Laxmi would urge. "You mustn't lose your health." When she wasn't speaking to her cousin, she spoke to her husband, shorter conversations, in which she ended up arguing about whether to have chicken or lamb for dinner. "I'm sorry," Miranda heard her apologize at one point. "This whole thing just makes me a little paranoid."

Miranda and Dev didn't argue. They went to movies at the Nickelodeon and kissed the whole time. They ate pulled pork and cornbread in Davis Square, a paper napkin tucked like a cravat into the collar of Dev's shirt. They sipped sangria at the bar of a Spanish restaurant, a grinning pig's head presiding over their conversation. They went to the MFA and picked out a poster of water lilies for her bedroom. One Saturday, following an afternoon concert at Symphony Hall, he showed her his favorite place in the city, the Mapparium at the Christian Science center, where they stood inside a room made of glowing stained-glass panels, which was shaped like the inside of a globe, but looked like the outside of one. In the middle of the room was a transparent bridge, so that they felt as if they were standing in the center of the world. Dev pointed to India, which was red, and far more detailed than the map in *The Economist*. He explained that many of the countries, like Siam and Italian Somaliland, no longer existed in the same way; the names had changed by now. The ocean, as blue as a peacock's breast, appeared in two shades, depending on the depth of the water. He showed her the deepest spot on earth, seven miles deep, above the Mariana Islands. They peered over the bridge and saw the Antarctic archipelago at their feet, craned their necks and saw a giant metal star overhead. As Dev spoke, his voice bounced wildly off the glass, sometimes loud, sometimes soft, sometimes seeming to land in Miranda's chest, sometimes eluding her ear altogether. When a group of tourists walked onto the bridge, she could hear them clearing their throats, as if through microphones. Dev explained that it was because of the acoustics.

Miranda found London, where Laxmi's cousin's husband was, with the woman he'd met on the plane. She wondered which of the cities in India Dev's wife was in. The farthest Miranda had ever been was to the Bahamas once when she was a child. She searched but couldn't find it on the glass panels. when the tourists left and she and Dev were alone again, he told her to stand at one end of the bridge. Even though they were thirty feet apart, Dev said, they'd be able to hear each other whisper.

"I don't believe you," Miranda said. It was the first time she'd spoken since they'd entered. She felt as if speakers were embedded in her ears.

"Go ahead," he urged, walking backward to his end of the bridge. His voice dropped to a whisper. "Say something." She watched his lips forming the words; at the same time she heard them so clearly that she felt them under her skin, under her winter coat, so near and full of warmth that she felt herself go hot.

"Hi," she whispered, unsure of what else to say.

"You're sexy," he whispered back.

At work the following week, Laxmi told Miranda that it wasn't the first time her cousin's husband had an affair. "She's decided to let him come to his senses," Laxmi said one evening as they were getting ready to leave the office. "She says it's for the boy. She's willing to forgive him for the boy." Miranda waited as Laxmi shut off her computer. "He'll come crawling back, and she'll let him," Laxmi said, shaking her head. "Not me. If my husband so much as looked at another woman I'd change the locks." She studied the picture tacked to her cubicle. Laxmi's husband had his arm draped over her shoulder, his knees learning in toward her on the bench. She turned to Miranda. "Wouldn't you?"

She nodded. Dev's wife was coming back from India the next day. That afternoon he'd called Miranda at work, to say he had to go to the airport to pick her up. He promised he'd call as soon as he could.

"What's the Taj Mahal like?" she asked Laxmi.

"The most romantic spot on earth." Laxmi's face brightened at the memory. "An everlasting monument to love."

While Dev was at the airport, Miranda went to Filenes's Basement to buy herself things she thought a mistress should have. She found a pair of black high heels with buckles smaller than a baby's teeth. She found a satin slip with scalloped edges and a knee-length silk robe. Instead of the pantyhose she normally wore to work, she found sheer stockings with a seam. She searched through piles and wandered through racks, pressing back hanger after hanger, until she found a cocktail dress made of a slinky silvery material that matched her eyes, with little chains for straps. As she shopped she thought about Dev, and about what he'd told her in the Mapparium. It was the first time a man had called her sexy, and when she closed her eyes she could still feel his whisper drifting through her body, under her skin. In the fitting room, which was just one big room with mirrors on the walls, she found a spot next to an older woman with a shiny face and coarse frosted hair. The woman stood barefoot in her underwear. pulling the black net of a body stocking taut between her fingers.

"Always check for snags," the woman advised.

Miranda pulled out the satin slip with scalloped edges. She held it to her chest.

The woman nodded with approval. "Oh yes."

"And this?" She held up the silver cocktail dress.

"Absolutely," the woman said. "He'll want to rip it right off you."

Miranda pictured the two of them at a restaurant in the South End they'd been to, where Dev had ordered foie gras and a soup made with champagne and raspberries. She pictured herself in the cocktail dress, and Dev in one of his suits, kissing her hand across the table. Only the next time Dev came to visit her, on a Sunday afternoon several days since the last time they'd seen each other, he was in gym clothes. After his wife came back, that was his excuse: on Sundays he drove into Boston and went running along the Charles. The first Sunday she opened the door in the knee-length robe, but Dev didn't even notice it; he carried her over to the bed, wearing sweatpants and sneakers, and entered her without a word. Later, she slipped on the robe when she walked across the room to get him a saucer for his cigarette ashes, but he complained that she was depriving him of the sight of her long legs, and demanded that she remove it. So the next Sunday she didn't bother. She wore jeans. She kept the lingerie at the back of a drawer, behind her socks and everyday underwear. The silver cocktail. dress hung in her closet, the tag dangling from the seam. Often, in the morning, the dress would be in a heap on the floor; the chain straps always slipped off the metal hanger.

Still, Miranda looked forward to Sundays. In the mornings she went to a deli and bought a baguette and little containers of things Dev liked to eat, like pickled herring, and potato salad, and tortes of pesto and mascarpone cheese. They ate in bed, picking up the herring with their fingers and ripping the baguette with their hands. Dev told her stories about his childhood, when he would come home from school and drink mango juice served to him on a tray, and then play cricket by a lake, dressed all in white. He told her about how, at eighteen, he'd been sent to a college in upstate New York during something called the Emergency, and about how it took him years to be able to follow American accents in movies, in spite of the fact that he'd had an English-medium education. As he talked he smoked three cigarettes, crushing them in a saucer by the side of her bed. Sometimes he asked her questions, like how many lovers she'd had (three) and how old she'd been the first time (nineteen). After lunch they made love, on sheets covered with crumbs and then Dev took a nap for twelve minutes. Miranda had never known an adult who took naps, but Dev said it was something he'd grown up doing in India, where it was so hot that people didn't leave their homes until the sun went down. "Plus it allows us to sleep together," he murmured mischievously, curving his arm like a big bracelet around her body.

Only Miranda never slept. She watched the clock on her bedside table, or pressed her face against Dev's fingers, intertwined with hers, each with its half-dozen hairs at the knuckle. After six minutes she turned to face him, sighing and stretching, to test if he was really sleeping. He always was. His ribs were visible through his skin as he breathed, and yet he was beginning to develop a paunch. He complained about the hair on his shoulders, but Miranda thought him perfect, and refused to imagine him any other way.

At the end of twelve minutes Dev would open his eyes as if he'd been awake all along, smiling at her, full of a contentment she wished she felt herself. "The best twelve minutes of the week," He'd sigh, running a hand along the backs of her calves. Then he'd spring out of bed, pulling on his sweatpants and lacing up his sneakers. He would go to the bathroom and brush his teeth with his index finger, something he told her all Indians knew how to do, to get rid of the smoke in his mouth. When she kissed him good-bye she smelled herself sometimes in his hair. But she knew that his excuse, that he'd spent the afternoon jogging, allowed him to take a shower when he got home, first thing.

Apart from Laxmi and Dev, the only Indians whom Miranda had known were a family in the neighborhood where she'd grown up, named the Dixits. Much to the amusement of the neighborhood children, including Miranda, but not including the Dixit children, Mr. Dixit would jog each evening along the flat winding streets of their development in his everyday shirt and trousers, his only concession to athletic apparel a pair of cheap Keds. Every weekend, the family—mother, father, two boys, and a girl—piled into their car and went away, to where nobody knew. The fathers complained that Mr. Dixit did not fertilize his lawn properly, did not rake his leaves on time, and agreed that the Dixits' house, the only one with vinyl siding, detracted from the neighborhood's charm. The mothers never invited Mrs. Dixit to join them around the Armstrongs' swimming pool. Waiting for the school bus with the Dixit children standing to one side, the other children would say "The Dixits dig shit," under their breath, and then burst into laughter.

One year, all the neighborhood children were invited to the birthday party of the Dixit girl. Miranda remembered a heavy aroma of incense and onions in the house, and a pile of shoes heaped by the front door. But most of all she remembered a piece of fabric, about the size of a pillowcase, which hung from a wooden dowel at the bottom of the stairs. It was a painting of a naked woman with a red face shaped like a knight's shield. She had enormous white eyes that tilted towards her temples, and mere dots for pupils. Two circles, with the same dots at their centers, indicated her breasts. In one hand she brandished a dagger. With one foot she crushed a struggling man on the ground. Around her body was a necklace composed of bleeding heads, strung together like a popcorn chain. She stuck her tongue out at Miranda.

"It is the goddess Kali," Mrs. Dixit explained brightly, shifting the dowel slightly in order to straighten the image. Mrs. Dixit's hands were painted with henna, an intricate pattern of zigzags and stars. "Come please, time for cake."

Miranda, then nine years old, had been too frightened to eat the cake. For months afterward she'd been too frightened even to walk on the same side of the street as the Dixits' house, which she had to pass twice daily, once to get to the bus stop, and once again to come home. For a while she even held her breath until she reached the next lawn, just as she did when the school bus passed a cemetery.

It shamed her now. Now, when she and Dev made love, Miranda closed her eyes and saw deserts and elephants, and marble pavilions floating on lakes beneath a full moon. One Saturday, having nothing else to do, she walked all the way to Central Square, to an Indian restaurant, and ordered a plate of tandoori chicken. As she ate she tried to memorize phrases printed at the bottom of the menu, for things like "delicious" and "water" and "check, please." The phrases didn't stick in her mind, and so she began to stop from time to time in the foreign-language section of a bookstore in Kenmore Square, where she studied the Bengali alphabet in the Teach Youself series. Once she went so far as to try to transcribe the Indian part of her name. "Mira," into her Filofax, her hand moving in unfamiliar directions, stopping and turning and picking up her pen when she least expected to. Following the arrows in the book, she drew a bar from left to right from which the letters hung; one looked more like a number than a letter, another looked like a triangle on its side. It had taken her several tries to get the letters of her name to resemble the sample letters in the book, and even then she wasn't sure if she'd written Mira or Mara. It was a scribble to her, but somewhere in the world, she realized with a shock, it meant something.

During the week it wasn't so bad. Work kept her busy, and she and Laxmi had begun having lunch together at a new Indian restaurant around the corner, during which Laxmi reported the latest status of her cousin's marriage. Sometimes Miranda tried to change the topic; it made her feel the way she once felt in college, when she and her boyfriend at the time had walked away from a crowded house of pancakes without paying for their food, just to see if they could get away with it. But Laxmi spoke of nothing else. "If I were her I'd fly straight to London and shoot them both," she announced one day. She snapped a papadum in half and dipped it into chutney. "I don't know how she can just wait this way."

Miranda knew how to wait. In the evenings she sat at her dining table and coated her nails with clear nail polish, and ate salad straight from the salad bowl, and watched television, and waited for Sunday. Saturdays were the worst because by Saturday it seemed that Sunday would never come. One Saturday when Dev called, late at night, she heard people laughing and talking in the background, so many that she asked him if he was at a concert hall. But he was only calling from his house in the suburbs. "I can't hear you that well," he said. "We have guests. Miss me?" She looked at the television screen, a sitcom that she'd muted with the remote control when the phone rang. She pictured him whispering into his cell phone, in a room upstairs, a hand on the doorknob, the hallway filled with guests. "Miranda, do you miss me?" he asked again. She told him that she did.

The next day, when Dev came to visit, Miranda asked him what his wife looked like. She was nervous to ask, waiting until he'd smoked the last of his cigarettes, crushing it with a firm twist into the saucer. She wondered if they'd quarrel. But Dev wasn't surprised by the question. He told her, spreading some smoked whitefish on a cracker, that his wife resembled an actresss in Bombay named Madhuri Dixit.

For an instant Miranda's heart stopped. But no. the Dixit girl had been named something else, something that began with P. Still, she wondered if the actress and the Dixit girl were related. She'd been plain, wearing her hair in two braids all through high school.

A few days later Miranda went to an Indian grocery in Central Square which also rented videos. The door opened to a complicated tinkling of bells. It was dinnertime, and she was the only customer. A video was playing on a television hooked up in a corner of the store: a row of young women in harem pants were thrusting their hips in synchrony on a beach.

"Can I help you?" the man standing at the cash register asked. He was eating a samosa, dipping it into some dark brown sauce on a paper plate. Below the glass counter at his waist were trays of more plump samosas, and what looked like pale, diamond-shaped pieces of fudge covered with foil, and some bright orange pastries floating in syrup. "You like some video?"

Miranda opened up her Filofax, where she had written "Mottery Dixit." She looked up at the videos on the shelves behind the counter. She saw women wearing skirts that sat low on the hips and tops that tied like bandannas between their breasts. Some leaned back against a stone wall, or a tree. They were beautiful, the way the women dancing on the beach were beautiful, with kohl-rimmed eyes and long black hair. She knew then that Madhuri Dixit was beautiful, too.

"We have subtitled versions, miss," the man continued. He wiped his fingertips quickly on his shirts and pulled out three titles.

"No," Miranda said. "Thank you, no." She wandered through the store, studying shelves lined with unlabeled packets and tins. The freezer case was stuffed with bags of pita bread and vegetables she didn't recognize. The only thing she recognized was a rack lined with bags and bags of the Hot Mix that Laxmi was always eating. She thought about buying some for Laxmi, then hesitated, wondering how to explain what she'd been doing in an Indian grocery.

"Very spicy," the man said, shaking his head, his eyes traveling across Miranda's body. "Too spicy for you."

By February, Laxmi's cousin's husband still hadn't come to his senses. He had returned to Montreal, argued bitterly with his wife for two weeks, packed two suitcases, and flown back to London. He wanted a divorce.

Miranda sat in her cubicle and listened as Laxmi kept telling her cousin that there were better men in the world, just waiting to come out of the woodwork. The next day the cousin said she and her son were going to her parents' house in California, to try to recuperate. Laxmi convinced her to arrange a weekend layover in Boston. "A quick change of place will do you good," Laxmi insisted gently, "besides which, I haven't seen you in years."

Miranda stared at her own phone, wishing Dev would call. It had been four days since their last conversation. She heard Laxmi dialing directory assitance, asking for the number of a beauty salon. "Something soothing," Laxmi requested. She scheduled massages, facials, manicures, and pedicures. Then she reserved a table for lunch at the Four Seasons. In her determination to cheer up her cousin, Laxmi had forgotten about the boy. She rapped her knuckles on the laminated wall.

"Are you busy Saturday?"

The boy was thin. He wore a yellow knapsack strapped across his back, gray herringbone trousers, a red V-necked sweater, and black leather shoes. His hair was cut in a thick fringe over his eyes, which had dark circles under them. They were the first thing Miranda noticed. They made him look haggard, as if he smoked a great deal and slept very little, in spite of the fact that he was only seven years old. He clasped a large sketch pad with a spiral binding. His name was Rohin.

"Ask me a capital," he said, staring up at Miranda.

She stared back at him. It was eight-thirty on a Saturday morning. She took a sip of coffee. "A what?"

"It's a game he's been playing," Laxmi's cousin explained. She was thin like her son, with a long face and the same dark circles under her eyes. A rust-colored coat hung heavy on her shoulders. Her black hair, with a few strands of gray at the temples, was pulled back like a ballerina's. "You ask him a country and he tells you the capital."

"You should have heard him in the car," Laxmi said. "He's already memorized all of Europe."

"It's not a game," Rohin said. "I'm having a competition with a boy at school. We're competing to memorize all the capitals. I'm going to beat him."

Miranda nodded. "Okay. What's the capital of India?"

"That's no good." He marched away, his arms swinging like a toy soldier. Then he marched back to Laxmi's cousin and tugged at a pocket of her overcoat. "Ask me a hard one."

"Senegal," she said.

"Dakar!" Rohin exclaimed triumphantly, and began running in larger and larger circles. Eventually he ran into the kitchen. Miranda could hear him opening and closing the fridge.

"Rohin, don't touch without asking," Laxmi's cousin called out wearily. She managed a smile for Miranda. "Don't worry, he'll fall asleep in a few hours. And thanks for watching him."

"Back at three," Laxmi said, disappearing with her cousin down the hallway. "We're double-parked."

Miranda fastened the chain on the door. She went to the kitchen to find Rohin, but he was now in the living room, at the dining table, kneeling on one of the director's chairs. He unzipped his knapsack, pushed Miranda's basket of manicure supplies to one side of the table, and spread his crayons over the surface. Miranda stood over his shoulder. She watched as he gripped a blue crayon and drew the outline of an airplane.

"It's lovely," she said. When he didn't reply, she went to the kitchen to pour herself more coffee.

"Some for me, please," Rohin called out.

She returned to the living room. "Some what?"

"Some coffee. There's enough in the pot. I saw."

She walked over to the table and sat opposite him. At times he nearly stood up to reach for a new crayon. He barely made a dent in the director's chair.

"You're too young for coffee."

Rohin leaned over the sketch pad, so that his tiny chest and shoulders almost touched it, his head tilted to one side. "The stewardess let me have coffee," he said. "She made it with milk and lots of sugar." He straightened, revealing a woman's face beside the plane, with long wavy hair and eyes like asterisks. "Her hair was more shiny," he decided, adding, "My father met a pretty woman on a plane, too." He looked at Miranda. His face darkened as he watched her sip. "Can't I have just a little coffee? Please?"

She wondered, in spite of his composed, brooding expression, if he were the type to throw a tantrum. She imagined his kicking her with his leather shoes, screaming for coffee, screaming and crying until his mother and Laxmi came back to fetch him. She went to the kitchen and prepared a cup for him as he'd requested. She selected a mug she didn't care for, in case he dropped it.

"Thank you," he said when she put it on the table. He took short sips, holding the mug securely with both hands.

Miranda sat with him while he drew, but when she attempted to put a coat of clear polish on her nails he protested. Instead he pulled out a paperback world almanac from his knapsack and asked her to quiz him. The countries were arranged by continent, six to a page, with the capitals in bold-face. followed by a short entry on the population, government, and other statistics. Miranda turned to a page in the Africa section and went down the list.

"Mali," she asked him.

"Bamako," he replied instantly.

"Malawi."

"Lilongwe."

She remembered looking at Africa in the Mapparium. She remembered the fat part of it was green.

"Go on," Rohin said.

"Mauritania."

"Nouakchott."

"Mauritius."

He paused, squeezed his eyes shut, then opened them, defeated. "I can't remember."

"Port Louis," she told him.

"Port Louis." He began to say it again and again, like a chant under his breath.

When they reached the last of the countries in Africa, Rohin said he wanted to watch cartoons, telling Miranda to watch them with him. When the cartoons ended, he followed her to the kitchen, and stood by her side as she made more coffee. He didn't follow her when she went to the bathroom a few minutes later, but when she opened the door she was startled to find him standing outside.

"Do you need to go?"

He shook his head but walked into the bathroom anyway. He put the cover of the toilet down, climbed on top of it, and surveyed the narrow glass shelf over the sink which held Miranda's toothbrush and makeup.

"What's this for?" he asked, picking up the sample of eye gel she'd gotten the day she met Dev.

"Puffiness."

"What's puffiness?"

"Here," she explained, pointing.

"After you've been crying?"

"I guess so."

Rohin opened the tube and smelled it. He squeezed a drop of it onto a finger, then rubbed it on his hand. "It stings." He inspected the back of his hand closely, as if expecting it to change color. "My mother has puffiness. She says it's a cold, but really she cries, sometimes for hours. Sometimes straight through dinner. Sometimes she cries so hard her eyes puff up like bullfrogs."

Miranda wondered if she ought to feed him. In the kitchen she discovered a bag of rice cakes and some lettuce. She offered to go out, to buy something from the deli, but Rohin said he wasn't very hungry, and accepted one of the rice cakes. "You eat one too," he said. They sat at the table, the rice cakes between them. He turned to a fresh page in his sketch pad.

"You draw."

She selected a blue crayon. "What should I draw?"

He thought for a moment. "I know," he said. He asked her to draw things in the living room: the sofa, the director's chairs, the television, the telephone. "This way I can memorize it."

"Memorize what?"

"Our day together." He reached for another rice cake.

"Why do you want to memorize it?"

"Because we're never going to see each other, ever again."

The precision of the phrase startled her. She looked at him, feeling slightly depressed. Rohin didn't look depressed. He tapped the page. "Go on."

And so she drew the items as best as she could—the sofa, the director's chairs, the television, the telephone. He sidled up to her, so close that it was sometimes difficult to see what she was doing. He put his small brown hand over hers. "Now me."

She handed him the crayon.

He shook his head. "No. now draw me."

"I can't," she said. "It won't look like you."

The brooding look began to spread across Rohin's face again, just as it had when she'd refused him coffee. "Please?"

She drew his face, outlining his head and the thick fringe of hair. He sat perfectly still, with a formal, melancholy expression, his gaze fixed to one side. Miranda wished she could draw a good likeness. Her hand moved in conjunction with her eyes, in unknown ways, just as it had that day in the bookstore when she'd transcribed her name in Bengali letters. It looked nothing like him. She was in the middle of drawing his nose when he wriggled away from the table.

"I'm bored." he announced, heading toward her bedroom. She heard him opening the door, opening the drawers of her bureau and closing them.

When she joined him he was inside the closet. After a moment he emerged, his hair disheveled, holding the silver cocktail dress. "This was on the floor."

"It falls off the hanger."

Rohin looked at the dress and then at Miranda's body. "Put it on."

"Excuse me?"

"Put it on."

There was no reason to put it on. Apart from in the fitting room at Filene's she had never worn it, and as long as she was with Dev she knew she never would. She knew they would never go to restaurants, where he would reach across a table and kiss her hand. They would meet in her apartment, on Sundays, he in his sweatpants, she in her jeans. She took the dress from Rohin and shook it out, even though the slinky fabric never wrinkled.She reached into the closet for a free hanger.

"Please put it on," Rohin asked, suddenly standing behind her. He pressed his face against her, clasping her waist with both his thin arms. "Please?"

"All right," she said, surprised by the strength of his grip.

He smiled, satisfied, and sat on the edge of her bed.

"You have to wait out there," she said, pointing to the door. "I'll come out when I'm ready."

"But my mother always takes her clothes off in front of me."

"She does?"

Rohin nodded. "She doesn't even pick them up afterward. She leaves them all on the floor by the bed, all tangled.

"One day she slept in my room." he continued. "She said it felt better than her bed, now that my father's gone."

"I'm not your mother," Miranda said, lifting him by the armpits off her bed. When he refused to stand, she picked him up. He was heavier than she expected, and he clung to her, his legs wrapped frimly around her hips, his head resting against her chest. She set him down in the hallway and shut the door. As an extra precaution she fastened the latch. She changed into the dress, glancing into the full-length mirror nailed to the back of the door. Her ankle socks looked silly, and so she opened a drawer and found the stockings. She searched through the back of the closet and slipped on the high heels with the tiny buckles. The chain straps of the dress were as light as paper clips against her collarbone. It was a bit loose on her. She could not zip it herself.

Rohin began knocking. "May I come in now?"

She opened the door. Rohin was holding his almanac in his hands, muttering something under his breath. His eyes opened wide at the sight of her. "I need help with the zipper," she said. She sat on the edge of the bed.

Rohin fastened the zipper to the top, and then Miranda stood up and twirled. Rohin put down the almanac. "You're sexy," he declared.

"What did you say?"

"You're sexy."

Miranda sat down again. Though she knew it meant nothing, her heart skipped a beat. Rohin probably referred to all women as sexy. He'd probably heard the word on television, or seen it on the cover of a magazine. She remembered the day in the Mapparium, standing across the bridge from Dev. At the time she thought she knew what his words meant. At the time they'd made sense.

Miranda folded her arms across her chest and looked Rohin in the eyes. "Tell me something."

He was silent.

"What does it mean?"

"What?"

"That word. 'Sexy.' What does it mean?"

He looked down, suddenly shy. "I can't tell you."

"Why not?"

"It's a secret." He pressed his lips together, so hard that a bit of them went white.

"Tell me the secret. I want to know."

Rohin sat on the bed beside Miranda and began to kick the edge of the mattress with the backs of his shoes. He giggled nervously, his thin body flinching as if it were being tickled.

"Tell me," Miranda demanded. She leaned over and gripped his ankles, holding his feet still.

Rohin looked at her, his eyes like slits. He struggled to kick the mattress again, but Miranda pressed against him. He fell back on the bed, his back straight as a board. He cupped his hands around his mouth, and then he whispered, "It means loving someone you don't know."

Miranda felt Rohin's words under her skin, the same way she'd felt Dev's. But instead of going hot she felt numb. It reminded her of the way she'd felt at the Indian grocery, the moment she knew, without even looking at a picture, that Madhuri Dixit, whom Dev's wife resembled, was beautiful.

"That's what my father did," Rohin continued. "He sat next to someone he didn't know, someone sexy, and now he loves her instead of my mother."

He took off his shoes and placed them side by side on the floor. Then he peeled back the comforter and crawled into Miranda's bed with the almanac. A minute later the book dropped from his hands, and he closed his eyes. Miranda watched him sleep, the comforter rising and falling as he breathed. He didn't wake up after twelve minutes like Dev, or even twenty. He didn't open his eyes as she stepped out of the silver cocktail dress and back into her jeans, and put the high-heeled shoes in the back of the closet, and rolled up the stockings and put them back in her drawer.

When she had put everything away she sat on the bed. She leaned toward him, close enough to see some white powder from the rice cakes stuck to the corners of his mouth, and picked up the almanac. As she turned the pages she imagined the quarrels Rohin had overheard in his house in Montreal. "Is she pretty?" his mother would have asked his father, wearing the same bathrobe she'd worn for weeks, her own pretty face turning spiteful. "Is she sexy?" His father would deny it at first, try to change the subject. "Tell me," Rohin's mother would shriek, "tell me if she's sexy." In the end his father would admit that she was, and his mother would cry and cry, in a bed surrounded by a tangle of clothes, her eyes puffing up like bull-frogs. "How could you," she'd ask, sobbing, "how could you love a woman you don't even know?"

As Miranda imagined the scene she began to cry a little herself. In the Mapparium that day, all the countries had seemed close enough to touch, and Dev's voice had bounced wildly off the glass. From across the bridge, thirty feet away, his words had reached her ears, so near and full of warmth that they'd drifted for days under her skin. Miranda cried harder, unable to stop. But Rohin still slept. She guessed that he was used to it now, to the sound of a woman crying.

On Sunday, Dev called to tell Miranda he was on his way. "I'm almost ready. I'll be there at two."

She was watching a cooking show on television. A woman pointed to a row of apples, explaining which were best for baking, "You shouldn't come today."

"Why not?"

"I have a cold," she lied. It wasn't far from the truth; crying had left her congested. "I've been in bed all morning."

"You do sound stuffed up." There was a pause. "Do you need anything?"

"I'm all set."

"Drink lots of fluids."

"Dev?"

"Yes, Miranda?"

"Do you remember that day we went to the Mapparium?"

"Of course."

"Do you remember how we whispered to each other?"

"I remember," Dev whispered playfully.

"Do you remember what you said?"

There was a pause. "Let's go back to your place." He laughed quietly. "Next Sunday, then?"

The day before, as she'd cried. Miranda had believed she would never forget anything—not even the way her name looked written in Bengali. She'd fallen asleep beside Rohin and when she woke up he was drawing an airplane on the copy of *The Economist* she'd saved, hidden under the bed. "Who's Devajit Mitra?" he had asked, looking at the address label.

Miranda pictured Dev, in his sweatpants and sneakers, laughing into the phone. In a moment he'd join his wife downstairs, and tell her he wasn't going jogging. He'd pulled a muscle while stretching, he'd say, settling down to read the paper. In spite of herself, she longed for him. She would see him one more Sunday, she decided, perhaps two. Then she would tell him the things she had known all along: that it wasn't fair to her, or to his wife, that they both deserved better, that there was no point in it dragging on.

But the next Sunday it snowed, so much so that Dev couldn't tell his wife he was going running along the Charles. The Sunday after that, the snow had melted, but Miranda made plans to go to the movies with Laxmi, and when she told Dev this over the phone, he didn't ask her to cancel them. The third Sunday she got up early and went out for a walk. It was cold but sunny, and so she walked all the way down Common-wealth Avenue, past the restaurants where Dev had kissed her, and then she walked all the way to the Christian Science center. The Mapparium was closed, but she bought a cup of coffee nearby and sat on one of the benches in the plaza outside the church, gazing at its giant pillars and its massive dome, and at the clear-blue sky spread over the city.

□

13. INTERPRETER OF MALADIES

(Jhumpa Lahiri)

AT THE TEA STALL Mr. and Mrs. Das bickered about who should take Tina to the toilet. Eventually Mrs. Das relented when Mr. Das pointed out that he had given the girl her bath the night before. In the rearview mirror Mr. Kapasi watched as Mrs. Das emerged slowly from his bulky white Ambassador, dragging her shaved, largely bare legs across the back seat. She did not hold the little girl's hand as they walked to the rest room.

They were on their way to see the Sun Temple at Konarak. It was a dry, bright Saturday, the mid-July heat tempered by a steady ocean breeze, ideal weather for sightseeing. Ordinarily Mr. Kapasi would not have stopped so soon along the way, but less than five minutes after he'd picked up the family that morning in front of Hotel Sandy Villa, the little girl had complained. The first thing Mr. Kapasi had noticed when he saw Mr. and Mrs. Das, standing with their children under the portico of the hotel, was that they were very young, perhaps not even thirty. In addition to Tina they had two boys, Ronny and Bobby, who appeared very close in age and had teeth covered in a network of flashing silver wires. The family looked Indian but dressed as foreigners did, the children in stiff, brightly colored clothing and caps with translucent visors. Mr. Kapasi was accustomed to foreign tourists; he was assigned to them regularly because he could speak English. Yesterday he had driven an elderly couple from Scotland, both with spotted faces and fluffy white hair so thin it exposed their sunburnt scalps. In comparison, the tanned, youthful faces of Mr. and Mrs. Das were all the more striking. When he'd introduced himself, Mr. Kapasi had pressed his palms together in greeting, but Mrs. Das squeezed hands like an American so that Mr. Kapasi felt it in his elbow. Mrs. Das, for her part, had flexed one side of her mouth, smiling dutifully at Mr. Kapasi, without displaying any interest in him.

As they waited at the tea stall, Ronny, who looked like the older of the two boys, clambered suddenly out of the back seat, intrigued by a goat tied to a stake in the ground.

"Don't touch it," Mr. Das said. He glanced up from his paperback tour book, which said "INDIA" in yellow letters and looked as if it had been published abroad. His voice, somehow tentative and a little shrill, sounded as though it had not yet settled into maturity.

"I want to give it a piece of gum," the boy called back as he trotted ahead.

Mr. Das stepped out of the car and stretched his legs by squatting briefly to the ground. A clean-shaven man, he looked exactly like a magnified version of Ronny. He had a sapphire blue visor, and was dressed in shorts, sneakers, and a T-shirt. The camera slung around his neck, with an impressive telephoto lens and numerous buttons and markings, was the only complicated thing he wore. He frowned, watching as Ronny rushed toward the goat, but appeared to have no intention of intervening. "Bobby, make sure that your brother doesn't do anything stupid."

"I don't feel like it," Bobby said, not moving. He was sitting in the front seat beside Mr. Kapasi, studying a picture of the elephant god taped to the glove compartment.

"No need to worry," Mr. Kapasi said. "They are quite tame." Mr. Kapasi was forty-six years old, with receding hair that had gone completely silver, but his butterscotch complexion and his unlined brow, which he treated in spare moments to dabs of lotus-oil balm, made it easy to imagine what he must have looked like at an earlier age. He wore gray trousers and a matching jacket-style shirt, tapered at the waist, with short sleeves and a large pointed collar, made of a thin but durable synthetic material. He had specified both the cut and the fabric to his tailor—it was his preferred uniform for giving tours because it did not get crushed during his long hours behind the wheel. Through the windshield he watched as Ronny circled around the goat, touched it quickly on its side, then trotted back to the car.

"You left India as a child?" Mr. Kapasi asked when Mr. Das had settled once again into the passenger seat.

"Oh, Mina and I were both born in America," Mr. Das announced with an air of sudden confidence. "Born and raised. Our parents live here now, in Assansol. They retired. We visit them every couple years." He turned to watch as the little girl ran toward the car, the wide purple bows of her sundress flopping on her narrow brown shoulders. She was holding to her chest a doll with yellow hair that looked as if it had been chopped, as a punitive measure, with a pair of dull scissors. "This is Tina's first trip to India, isn't it, Tina?"

"I don't have to go to the bathroom anymore." Tina announced.

"Where's Mina?" Mr. Das asked.

Mr. Kapasi found it strange that Mr. Das should refer to his wife by her first name when speaking to the little girl. Tina pointed to where Mrs. Das was purchasing something from one of the shirtless men who worked at the tea stall. Mr. Kapasi heard one of the shirtless men sing a phrase from a popular Hindi love song as Mrs. Das walked back to the car, but she did not appear to understand the words of the song, for she did not express irritation, or embarrassment, or react in any other way to the man's declarations.

He observed her. She wore a red-and-white-checkered skirt that stopped above her knees, slip-on shoes with a square wooden heel, and a close-fitting blouse styled like a man's undershirt. The blouse was decorated at chest-level with a calico applique' in the shape of a strawberry. She was a short woman, with small hands like paws, her frosty pink finger-nails painted to match her lips, and was slightly plump in her figure. Her hair, shorn only a little longer than her husband's, was parted far to one side. She was wearing large dark brown sunglasses with a pinkish tint to them, and carried a big straw bag, almost as big as her torso, shaped like a bowl, with a water bottle poking out of it. She walked slowly, carrying some puffed rice tossed with peanuts and chili peppers in a large packet made from newspapers. Mr. Kapasi turned to Mr. Das.

"Where in America do you live?"

"New Brunswick, New Jersey."

"Next to New York?"

"Exactly. I teach middle school there."

"What subject?"

"Science. In fact, every year I take my students on a trip to the Museum of Natural History in New York City. In a way we have a lot in common, you could say, you and I. How long have you been a tour guide, Mr. Kapasi?"

"Five years."

Mrs. Das reached the car. "How long's the trip?" she asked, shutting the door.

"About two and a half hours," Mr. Kapasi replied.

At this Mrs. Das gave an impatient sigh, as if she had been traveling her whole life without pause. She fanned herself with a folded Bombay film magazine written in English.

"I thought that the Sun Temple is only eighteen miles north of Puri," Mr. Das said, tapping on the tour book.

"The roads to Konarak are poor. Actually it is a distance of fifty-two miles," Mr. Kapasi explained.

Mr. Das nodded, readjusting the camera strap where it had begun to chafe the back of his neck.

Before starting the ignition, Mr. Kapasi reached back to make sure the cranklike locks on the inside of each of the back doors were secured. As soon as the car began to move the little girl began to play with the lock on her side, clicking it with some effort forward and backward, but Mrs. Das said nothing to stop her. She sat a bit slouched at one end of the back seat, not offering her puffed rice to anyone. Ronny and Tina sat on either side of her, both snapping bright green gum.

"Look," Bobby said as the car began to gather speed. He pointed with his finger to the tall trees that lined the road.

"Look."

"Monkeys!" Ronny shrieked. "Wow!"

They were seated in groups along the branches, with shining black faces, silver bodies, horizontal eyebrows, and crested heads. Their long gray tails dangled like a series of ropes among the leaves. A few scratched themselves with black leathery hands, or swung their feet, staring as the car passed.

"We call them the hanuman," Mr. Kapasi said. "They are quite common in the area."

As soon as he spoke, one of the monkeys leaped into the middle of the road, causing Mr. Kapasi to brake suddenly. Another bounced onto the hood of the car, then sprang away. Mr. Kapasi beeped his horn. The children began to get excited, sucking in their breath and covering their faces partly with their hands. They had never seen monkeys outside of a zoo, Mr. Das explained. He asked Mr. Kapasi to stop the car so that he could take a picture.

While Mr. Das adjusted his telephoto lens, Mrs. Das reached into her straw bag and pulled out a bottle of colorless nail polish, which she proceeded to stroke on the tip of her index finger.

The little girl stuck out a hand. "Mine too. Mommy, do mine too."

"Leave me alone," Mrs. Das said, blowing on her nail and turning her body slightly. "You're making me mess up."

The little girl occupied herself by buttoning and unbuttoning a pinafore on the doll's plastic body.

"All set," Mr. Das said, replacing the lens cap.

The car rattled considerably as it raced along the dusty road, causing them all to pop up from their seats every now and then, but Mrs. Das continued to polish her nails. Mr. Kapasi eased up on the accelerator, hoping to produce a smoother ride. When he reached for the gearshift the body in front accommodated him by swinging his hairless knees out of the way. Mr. Kapasi noted that this boy was slightly paler than the other children. "Daddy, why is the driver sitting on the wrong side in this car, too?" the boy asked.

"They all do that here, dummy," Ronny said.

"Don't call your brother a dummy," Mr. Das said. He turned to Mr. Kapasi. "In America, you know ... it confuses them."

"Oh yes, I am well aware," Mr. Kapasi said. As delicately as he could, he shifted gears again, accelerating as they approached a hill in the road. "I see it on *Dallas*, the steering wheels are on the left-hand side."

"What's *Dallas?*" Tina asked, banging her now naked doll on the seat behind Mr. Kapasi.

"It went off the air," Mr. Das explained. "It's a television show."

They were all like siblings, Mr. Kapasi thought as they passed a row of date trees. Mr. and Mrs. Das behaved like an older brother and sister, not parents. It seemed that they were in charge of the children only for the day; it was hard to believe they were regularly responsible for anything other than themselves. Mr. Das tapped on his lens cap, and his tour book, dragging his thumbnail occasionally across the pages so that they made a scraping sound. Mrs. Das continued to polish her nails. She had still not removed her sunglasses. Every now and then Tina renewed her plea that she wanted her nails done, too. and so at one point Mrs. Das flicked a drop of polish on the little girl's finger before depositing the bottle back inside her straw bag.

"Isn't this an air-conditioned car?" she asked, still blowing on her hand. The window on Tina's side was broken and could not be rolled down.

"Quit complaining," Mr. Das said. "It isn't so hot."

"I told you to get a car with air-conditioning," Mrs. Das continued. "Why do you do this, Raj, just to save a few stupid rupees. What are you saving us, fifty cents?"

Their accents sounded just like the ones Mrs. Kapasi heard on American television programs, though not like the ones on *Dallas.*

"Doesn't it get tiresome, Mr. Kapasi, showing people the same thing every day?" Mr. Das asked, rolling down his own window all the way. "Hey, do you mind stopping the car. I just want to get a shot of this guy."

Mr. Kapasi pulled over to the side of the road as Mr. Das took a picture of a barefoot man, his head wrapped in a dirty turban. seated on top of a cart of grain sacks pulled by a pair of bullocks. Both the man and the bullocks were emaciated. In the back seat Mrs. Das gazed out another window, at the sky, where nearly transparent clouds passed quickly in front of one another.

"I look forward to it, actually," Mr. Kapasi said as they continued on their way. "The Sun Temple is one of my favourite places. In that way it is a reward for me. I give tours on Fridays and Saturdays only. I have another job during the week."

"Oh? Where?" Mr. Das asked.

"I work in a doctor's office."

"You're a doctor?"

"I am not a doctor. I work with one. As an interpreter."

"What does a doctor need an interpreter for?"

"He has a number of Gujarati patients. My father was Gujarati, but many people do not speak Gujarati in this area, including the doctor. And so the doctor asked me to work in his office, interpreting what the patients say."

"Interesting. I've never heard of anything like that," Mr. Das said.

Mr. Kapasi shrugged. "It is a job like any other."

"But so romantic," Mrs. Das said dreamily, breaking her extended silence. She lifted her pinkish brown sunglasses and arranged them on top of her head like a tiara. For the first time, her eyes met Mr. Kapasi's in the rearview mirror : pale, a bit small, their gaze fixed but drowsy.

Mr. Das craned to look at her. "What's so romatic about it?"

"I don't know. Something." She shrugged, knitting her brows together for an instant. "Would you like a piece of gum. Mr. Kapasi?" she asked brightly. She reached into her straw bag and handed him a small square wrapped in green-and-white-striped paper. As soon as Mr. Kapasi put the gum in his mouth a thick sweet liquid burst onto his tongue.

"Tell us more about your job, Mr. Kapasi," Mrs. Das said.

"What would you like to know, madame?"

"I don't know," she shrugged, munching on some puffed rice and licking the mustard oil from the corners of her mouth. "Tell us a typical situation." She settled back in her seat, her head tilted in a patch of sun, and closed her eyes. "I want to picture what happens."

"Very well. The other day a man came in with a pain in his throat."

"Did he smoke cigarettes?"

"No. It was very curious. He complained that he felt as if there were long pieces of straw stuck in his throat. When I told the doctor he was able to prescribe the proper medication."

"That's so neat."

"Yes," Mr. Kapasi agreed after some hesitation.

"So these patients are totally dependent on you," Mrs. Das said. She spoke slowly, as if she were thinking aloud. "In a way, more dependent on you than the doctor."

"How do you mean? How could it be?"

"Well, for example, you could tell the doctor that the pain felt like a burning, not straw. The patient would never know what you had told the doctor, and the doctor wouldn't know that you had told the wrong thing. It's a big responsibility."

"Yes, a big responsibility you have there, Mr. Kapasi," Mr. Das agreed.

Mr. Kapasi had never thought of his job in such complimentary terms. To him it was a thankless occupation. He found nothing noble in interpreting people's maladies, assiduously translating the symptoms of so many swollen bones, countless cramps of bellies and bowels, spots on people's palms that changed color, shape, or size. The doctor, nearly half his age, had an affinity for bell-bottom trousers and made humorless jokes about the Congress party. Together they worked in a stale little infirmary where Mr. Kapasi's smartly tailored clothes clung to him in the heat, in spite of the blackened blades of a ceiling fan churning over their heads.

The job was a sign of his failings. In his youth he'd been a devoted scholar of foreign languages, the owner of an impressive collection of dictionaries. He had dreamed of being an interpreter for diplomats and dignitaries, resolving conflicts between people and nations, settling disputes of which he along could understand both sides. He was a self-educated man. In a series of notebooks, in the evenings before his parents settled his marriage, he had listed the common etymologies of words, and at one point in his life he was confident that he could converse, if given the opportunity, in English. French, Russion, Portuguese, and Italian, not to mention Hindi, Bengali, Orissi, and Gujarati. Now only a handful of European phrases remained in his memory, scattered words for things like saucers and chairs. English was the only non-Indian language he spoke fluently anymore. Mr. Kapasi knew it was not a remarkable talent. Sometimes he feared that his children knew better English than he did, just from watching television. Still, it came in handy for the tours.

He had taken the job as an interpreter after his first son, at the age of seven, contracted typhoid—that was how he had first made the acquaintance of the doctor. At the time Mr. Kapasi had been teaching English in a grammar school, and he bartered his skills as an interpreter to pay the increasingly exorbitant medical bills. In the end the boy had died one evening in his mother's arms. his limbs burning with fever, but then there was the funeral to pay for, and the other children who were born soon enough, and the newer, bigger house, and the good schools and tutors, and the fine shoes and the television, and the countless other ways he tried to console his wife and to keep her from crying in her sleep, and so when the doctor offered to pay him twice as much as he earned at the grammar school, he accepted. Mr. Kapasi knew that his wife had little regard for his career as an interpreter. He knew it reminded her of the son she'd lost, and that she resented the other lives he helped, in his own small way, to save. If ever she referred to his position, she used the phrase "doctor's assistant," as if the process of interpretation were equal to taking someone's temperature, or changing a bedpan. She never asked him about the patients who came to the doctor's office, or said that his job was a big responsibility.

For this reason it flattered Mr. Kapasi that Mrs. Das was so intrigued by his job. Unlike his wife, she had reminded him of its intellectual challenges. She had also used the word "romantic." She did not behave in a romantic way toward her husband, and yet she had used the word to describe him. He wondered if Mr. and Mrs. Das were a bad match, just as he and his wife were. Perhaps they, too, had little in common apart from three children and a decade of their lives. The signs he recognized from his own marriage were there—the bickering, the indifference, the protracted silences. Her sudden interest in him, an interest she did not express in either her husband or her children, was mildly intoxicating. When Mr. Kapasi thought once again about how she had said "romantic," the feeling of intoxication grew.

He began to check his reflection in the rearview mirror as he drove, feeling grateful that he had chosen the gray suit that morning, and not the brown one, which tended to sag a little in the knees. From time to time he glanced through the mirror at Mrs. Das. In addition to glancing at her face he glanced at the strawberry between her breasts, and the golden brown hollow in her throat. He decided to tell Mrs. Das about another patient, and another: the young woman who had complained of a sensation of raindrops in her spine, the gentleman whose birthmark had begun to sprout hairs. Mrs. Das listened attentively, stroking her hair with a small plastic brush that resembled an oval bed of nails, asking more questions, for yet another example. The children were quiet, intent on spotting more monkeys in the trees, and Mr. Das was absorbed by his tour book so it seemed like a private conversation between Mr. Kapasi and Mrs. Das. In this manner the next half hour passed, and when they stopped for lunch at a roadside restaurant that sold fritters and omelette sandwiches, usually something Mrs. Kapasi looked forward to on his tours so that he could sit in peace and enjoy some hot tea, he was disappointed. As the Das family settled together under a magenta umbrella fringed with white and orange tassels, and placed their orders with one of the waiters who marched about in tricornered caps, Mr. Kapasi reluctantly headed toward a neighboring table.

"Mr. Kapasi, wait. There's room here," Mrs. Das called out. She gathered Tina onto her lap, insisting that he accompany them. And so, together, they had bottled mango juice and sandwiches and plates of onions and potatoes deep-fried in graham-flour batter. After finishing two omelette sandwiches Mr. Das took more pictures of the group as they ate.

"How much longer?" he asked Mr. Kapasi as he paused to load a new roll of film in the camera.

"About half an hour more."

By now the children had gotten up from the table to look at more monkeys perched in a nearby tree, so there was a considerable space between Mrs. Das and Mr. Kapasi. Mr. Das placed the camera to his face and squeezed one eye shut, his tongue exposed at one corner of his mouth. "This looks funny. Mina, you need to lean in closer to Mr. Kapasi."

She did. He could smell a scent on her skin, like a mixture of whiskey and rosewater. He worried suddenly that she could smell his perspiration, which he knew had collected beneath the synthetic material of his shirt. He polished off his mango juice in one gulp and smoothed his silver hair with his hands. A bit of the juice dripped onto his chin. He wondered if Mrs. Das had noticed.

She had not. "What's your address, Mr. Kapasi?" she inquired, fishing for something inside her straw bag.

"You would like my address?"

"So we can send you copies," she said. "Of the pictures." She handed him a scrap of paper which she had hastily ripped from a page of her film magazine. The blank portion was limited, for the narrow strip was crowded by lines of text and a tiny picture of a hero and heroine embracing under a eucalyptus tree.

The paper curled as Mr. Kapasi wrote his address in clear, careful letters. She would write to him, asking about his days interpreting at the doctor's office, and he would respond eloquently, choosing only the most entertaining anecdotes, ones that would make her laugh out loud as she read them in her house in New Jersey. In time she would reveal the disappointment of her marriage, and he his. In this way their friendship would grow, and flourish. He would possess a picture of the two of them, eating fried onions under a magenta umbrella, which he would keep, he decided, safely tucked between the pages of his Russian grammar. As his mind raced, Mr. Kapasi experienced a mild and pleasant shock. It was similar to a feeling he used to experience long ago when, after months of translating with the aid of a dictionary, he would finally read a passage from a French novel, or an Italian sonnet, and understand the words, one after another, unencumbered by his own efforts. In those moments Mr. Kapasi used to believe that all was right with the world, that all struggles were rewarded, that all of life's mistakes made sense in the end. The promise that he would hear from Mrs. Das now filled him with the same belief.

When he finished writing his address Mr. Kapasi handed her the paper, but as soon as he did so he worried that he had either misspelled his name, or accidently reversed the numbers of his postal code. He dreaded the possibility of a lost letter, the photograph never reaching him, hovering somewhere in Orissa, close but ultimately unattainable. He thought of asking for the slip of paper again, just to make sure he had written his address accurately, but Mrs. Das had already dropped it into the jumble of her bag.

They reached Konarak at two-thirty. The temple, made of sandstone, was a massive pyramid-like structure in the shape of a chariot. It was dedicated to the great master of life, the sun, which struck three sides of the edifice as it made its journey each day across the sky. Twenty-four giant wheels were carved on the north and south sides of the plinth. The whole thing was drawn by a team of seven horses, speeding as if through the heavens. As they approached, Mr. Kapasi explained that the temple had been built between A. D. 1243 and 1255, with the efforts of twelve hundred artisans, by the great ruler of the Ganga dynasty, King Narasimhadeva the First, to commemorate his victory against the Muslim army.

"It says the temple occupies about a hundred and seventy acres of land," Mr. Das said, reading from his book.

"It's like a desert," Ronny said, his eyes wandering across the sand that stretched on all sides beyond the temple.

"The Chandrabhaga River once flowed one mile north of here. It is dry now," Mr. Kapasi said, turning off the engine.

They got out and walked toward the temple, posing first for pictures by the pair of lions that flanked the steps. Mr. Kapasi led them next to one of the wheels of the chariot, higher than any human being, nine feet in diameter.

"The wheels are supposed to symbolize the wheel of life," Mr. Das read. "They depict the cycle of creation, preservation, and achievement of realization, Cool." He turned the page of his book. "Each wheel is divided into eight thick and thin spokes, dividing the day into eight equal parts. The rims are carved with designs of birds and animals, whereas the medallions in the spokes are carved with women in luxurious poses, largely erotic in nature."

What he referred to were the countless friezes of entwined naked bodies, making love in various positions, women clinging to the necks of men, their knees wrapped eternally around their lovers' thighs. In addition to these were assorted scenes from daily life, of hunting and trading, of deer being killed with bows and arrows and marching warriors holding swords in their hands.

It was no longer possible to enter the temple, for it had filled with rubble years ago, but they admired the exterior, as did all the tourists Mr. Kapasi brought there, slowly strolling along each of its sides. Mr. Das trailed behind, taking pictures. The children ran ahead, pointing to figures of naked people, intrigued in particular by the Nagamithunas, the half-human, half-serpentine couples who were said, Mr. Kapasi told them, to live in the deepest waters of the sea. Mr. Kapasi was pleased that they liked the temple, pleased especially that it appealed to Mrs. Das. She stopped every three or four paces, staring silently at the carved lovers, and the processions of elephants, and the topless female musicians beating on two-sided drums.

Though Mr. Kapasi had been to the temple countless times, it occurred to him, as he, too, gazed at the topless women, that he had never seen his own wife fully naked. Even when they had made love she kept the panels of her blouse hooked together, the string of her petticoat knotted around her waist. He had never admired the backs of his wife's legs the way he now admired those of Mrs. Das, walking as if for his benefit alone. He had, of course, seen plenty of bare limbs before, belonging to the American and European ladies who took his tours. But Mrs. Das was different. Unlike the other women, who had an interest only in the temple, and kept their noses buried in a guidebook, or their eyes behind the lens of a camera, Mrs. Das had taken an interest in him.

Mr. Kapasi was anxious to be alone with her, to continue their private conversation, yet he felt nervous to walk at her side. She was lost behind her sunglasses, ignoring her husband's requests that she pose for another picture, walking past her children as if they were strangers. Worried that he might disturb her, Mr. Kapasi walked ahead, to admire, as he always did, the three life-sized bronze avatars of Surya, the sun god, each emerging from its own niche on the temple facade to greet the sun at down, noon, and evening. They wore elaborate headdresses, their languid, elongated eyes closed, their bare chests draped with carved chains and amulets. Hibiscus petals, offerings from previous visitors, were strewn at their gray-green feet. The last statue, on the northern wall of the temple, was Mr. Kapasi's favorite. This Surya had a tired expression weary after a hard day of work, sitting astride a horse with folded legs. Even his horse's eyes were drowsy. Around his body were smaller sculptures of women in pairs, their hips thrust to one side.

"Who's that?" Mrs. Das asked. He was stratled to see that she was standing beside him.

"He is the Astachala-Surya", Mr. Kapasi said. "The setting sun."

"So in a couple of hours the sun will set right here?" She slipped a foot out of one of her square-heeled shoes, rubbed her toes on the back of her other leg.

"That is correct."

She raised her sunglasses for a moment, then put them back on again. "Neat."

Mr. Kapasi was not certain exactly what the word suggested, but he had a feeling it was a favourable response. He hoped that Mrs. Das had understood Surya's beauty, his power. Perhaps they would discuss it further in their letters. He would explain things to her, things about India, and she would explain things to him about America. In its own way this correspondence would fulfill his dream, of serving as an interpreter between nations. He looked at her straw bag, delighted that his address lay nestled among its contents. When he pictured her so many thousands of miles away he plummeted, so much so that he had an overwhelming urge to wrap his arms around her, to freeze with her, even for an instant, in an embrace witnessed by his favorite Surya. But Mrs. Das had already started walking.

"When do you return to America?" he asked, trying to sound placid.

"In ten days."

He calculated: A week to settle in, a week to develop the pictures, a few days to compose her letter, two weeks to get to India by air.

According to his schedule, allowing room for delays, he would hear from Mrs. Das in approximately six weeks' time.

The family was silent as Mr. Kapasi drove them back, a little past four-thirty, to Hotel Sandy Villa. The children had bought miniature granite versions of the chariot's wheels at a souvenir stand, and they turned them round in their hands. Mr. Das continued to read his book. Mrs. Das untangled Tina's hair with her brush and divided it into two little ponytails.

Mr. Kapasi was beginning to dread the thought of dropping them off. He was not prepared to begin his six-week wait to hear from Mrs. Das. As he stole glances at her in the rearview mirror, wrapping elastic bands around Tina's hair, he wondered how he might make the tour a little longer. Ordinarily he sped back to Puri using a shortcut, eager to return home, scrub his feet and hands with sandalwood soap, and enjoy the evening newspaper and a cup of tea that his wife would serve him in silence. The thought of that silence, something to which he'd long been resigned, now oppressed him. It was then that he suggested visiting the hills at Udayagiri and Khandagiri, where a number of monastic dwellings were hewn out of the ground, facing one another across a defile. It was some miles away, but well worth seeing, Mr. Kapasi told them.

"Oh yeah, there's something mentioned about it in this book," Mr. Das said, "Built by a Jain king or something."

"Shall we go then?" Mr. Kapasi asked. He paused at a turn in the road. "It's to the left."

Mr. Das turned to look at Mrs. Das. Both of them shrugged. "Left, left." the children chanted.

Mr. Kapasi turned the wheel, almost delirious with relief. He did not know what he would do or say to Mrs. Das once they arrived at the hills. Perhaps he would tell her what a pleasing smile she had. Perhaps he would compliment her strawberry shirt. which he found irresistibly becoming. Perhaps, when Mr. Das was busy taking a picture, he would take her hand.

He did not have to worry. When they got to the hills, divided by a steep path thick with trees, Mrs. Das refused to get out of the car. All along the path, dozens of monkeys were seated on stones, as well as on the branches of the trees. Their hind legs were stretched out in front and raised to shoulder level, their arms resting on their knees.

"My legs are tired," she said, sinking low in her seat. "I'll stay here."

"Why did you have to wear those stupid shoes?" Mr. Das said. "You won't be in the pictures."

"Pretend I'm there."

"But we could use one of these pictures for our Christmas card this year. We didn't get one of all five of us at the Sun Temple. Mr.

Kapasi could take it."

"I'm not coming. Anyway, those monkeys give me the creeps."

"But they're harmless," Mr. Das said. He turned to Mr. Kapasi. "Aren't they?"

"They are more hungry than dangerous," Mr. Kapasi said. "Do not provoke them with food, and they will not bother you."

Mr. Das headed up the defile with the children, the boys at his side, the little girl on his shoulders. Mr. Kapasi watched as they crossed paths with a Japanese man and woman, the only other tourists there, who paused for a final photograph, then stepped into a nearby car and drove away. As the car disappeared out of view some of the monkeys called out, emitting soft whooping sounds, and then walked on their flat black hands and feet up the path. At one point a group of them formed a little ring around Mr. Das and the children. Tina screamed in delight. Ronny ran in circles around his father. Bobby bent down and picked up a fat stick on the ground. When he extended it, one of the monkeys approached him and snatched it, then briefly beat the ground.

"I'll join them," Mr. Kapasi said, unlocking the door on his side. "There is much to explain about the caves."

"No. Stay a minute," Mrs. Das said. She got out of the back seat and slipped in beside Mr. Kapasi. "Raj has his dumb book anyway." Together, through the windshield, Mrs. Das and Mr. Kapasi watched as Bobby and the monkey passed the stick back and forth between them.

"A brave little boy," Mr. Kapasi commented.

"It's not so surprising," Mrs. Das said.

"No?"

"He's not his."

"I beg your pardon?"

"Raj's. He's not Raj son."

Mr. Kapasi felt a prickle on his skin. He reached into his shirt pocket for the small tin of lotus-oil balm he carried with him at all times, and applied it to three spots on his forehead. He knew that Mrs. Das was watching him, but he did not turn to face her. Instead he watched as the figures of Mr. Das and the children grew smaller, climbing up the steep path, pausing every now and then for a picture, surrounded by a growing number of monkeys.

"Are you surprised?" The way she put it made him choose his words with care.

"It's not the type of thing one assumes," Mr. Kapasi replied slowly. He put the tin of lotus-oil balm back in his pocket.

"No, of course not. And no one knows, of course. No one at all. I've kept it a secret for eight whole years." She looked at Mr. Kapasi, tilting her chin as if to gain a fresh perspective. "But now I've told you."

Mr. Kapasi nodded. He felt suddenly parched, and his forehead was warm and slightly numb from the balm. He considered asking Mrs. Das for a sip of water, then decided against it.

"We met when we were very young," she said. She reached into her straw bag in search of something, then pulled out a packet of puffed rice. "Want some?"

"No, thank you."

She put a fistful in her mouth, sank into the seat a little, and looked away from Mr. Kapasi, out the window on her side of the car. "We married when we were still in college. We were in high school when he proposed. We went to the same college, of course. Back then we couldn't stand the thought of being separated not for a day, not for a minute. Our parents were best friends who lived in the same town. My entire life I saw him every weekend, either at our house or theirs. We were sent upstairs to play together while our parents joked about our marriage. Imagine! They never caught us at anything, though in a way I think it was all more or less a setup. The things we did those Friday and Saturday nights, while our parents sat downstairs drinking tea ... I could tell you stories, Mr. Kapasi."

As a result of spending all her time in college with Raj, she continued, she did not make many close friends. There was no one to confide in about him at the end of a difficult day, or to share a passing thought or a worry. Her parents now lived on the other side of the world, but she had never been very close to them, anyway. After marrying so young she was overwhelmed by it all, having a child so quickly, and nursing, and warming up bottles of milk and testing their temperature against her writst while Raj was at work, dressed in sweaters and corduroy pants, teaching his students about rocks and dinosaurs. Raj never looked cross or harried, or plump as she had become after the first baby.

Always tired, she declined invitations from her one or two college girlfriends, to have lunch or shop in Manhattan. Eventually the friends stopped calling her, so that she was left at home all day with the baby, surrounded by toys that made her trip when she walked or wince when she sat, always cross and tired. Only occasionally did they go out after Ronny was born, and even more rarely did they entertain. Raj didn't mind; he looked forward to coming home from teaching and watching television and bouncing Ronny on his knee. She had been outraged when Raj told her that a Punjabi friend, someone whom she had once met but did not remember, would be staying with them for a week for some job interviews in the New Brunswick area.

Bobby was conceived in the afternoon, on a sofa littered with rubber teething toys, after the friend learned that a London pharmaceutical company had hired him, while Ronny cried to be freed from his playpen. She made no protest when the friend touched the small of her back as she was about to make a pot of coffee, then pulled her against his crisp navy suit. He made love to her swiftly, in silence, with an expertise she had never known without the meaningful expressions and smiles Raj always insisted on afterward. The next day Raj drove the friend to JFK. He was married now, to a Punjabi girl, and they lived in London still, and every year they exchanged Christmas cards with Raj and Mina, each couple tucking photos of their families into the envelopes. He did not know that he was Bobby's father. He never would.

"I beg your pardon, Mrs. Das, but why have you told me this information?" Mr. Kapasi asked when she had finally finished speaking, and had turned to face him once again.

"For God's sake, stop calling me Mrs. Das. I'm twenty-eight. You probably have children my age."

"Not quite." It disturbed Mr. Kapasi to learn that she thought of him as a parent. The feeling he had had toward her, that had made him check his reflection in the rearview mirror as they drove, evaporated a little.

"I told you because of your talents." She put the packet of puffed rice back into her bag without folding over the top.

"I don't understand," Mr. Kapasi said.

"Don't you see? For eight years I haven't been able to express this to anybody, not to friends, certainly not to Raj. He doesn't even suspect it. He thinks I'm still in love with him. Well, don't you have anything to say?"

"About what?"

"About what I've just told you. About my secret, and about how terrible it makes me feel. I feel terrible looking at my children, and at Raj, always terrible. I have terrible urges, Mr. Kapasi, to throw things away. One day I had the urge to throw everything I own out the window, the television, the children, everything. Don't you think it's unhealthy?"

He was silent.

"Mr. Kapasi, don't you have anything to say? I thought that was your job."

"My job is to give tours, Mrs. Das."

"Not that. Your other job. As an interpreter."

"But we do not face a language barrier. What need is there for an interpreter?"

"That's not what I mean. I would never have told you otherwise. Don't you realize what it means for me to tell you?"

"What does it mean?"

"It means that I'm tired of feeling so terrible all the time. Eight years, Mr. Kapasi, I've been in pain eight years. I was hoping you could help me feel better, say the right thing. Suggest some kind of remedy."

He looked at her, in her red plaid skirt and strawberry T-shirt, a woman not yet thirty, who loved neither her husband nor her children, who had already fallen out of love with life. Her confession depressed him, depressed him all the more when he thought of Mr. Das at the top of the path, Tina clinging to his shoulders, taking pictures of ancient monastic cells cut into the hills to show his students in America, unsuspecting and unaware that one of his sons was not his own. Mr. Kapasi felt insulted that Mrs. Das should ask him to interpret her common, trivial little secret. She did not resemble the patients in the doctor's office, those who came glassy-eyed and desperate, unable to sleep or breathe or urinate with ease, unable, above all, to give words to their pains. Still, Mr. Kapasi believed it was his duty to assist Mrs. Das. Perhaps he ought to tell her to confess the truth to Mr. Das. He would explain that honesty was the best policy. Honesty, surely would help her feel better, as she'd put it. Perhaps he would offer to preside over the discussion, as a mediator. He decided to begin with the most obvious quesiton, to get to the heart of the matter, and so he asked, "Is it really pain you feel, Mrs. Das, or is it guilt?"

She turned to him and glared, mustard oil thick on her frosty pink lips, She opened her mouth to say something, but as she glared at Mrs. Kapasi some certain knowledge seemed to pass before her eyes, and she stopped. It crushed him; he knew at that moment that he was not even important enough to be properly insulted. She opened the car door and began walking up the path, wobbling a little on her square wooden heels, reaching into her straw bag to eat handfuls of puffed rice. It fell through her fingers, leaving a zigzagging trail, causing a monkey to leap down from a tree and devour the little white grains. In search of more, the monkey began to follow Mrs. Das. Others joined him, so that she was soon being followed by about half a dozen of them, their velvety tails dragging behind.

Mr. Kapasi stepped out of the car. He wanted to holler, to alert her in some way, but he worried that if she knew they were behind her, she would grow nervous. Perhaps she would lose her balance. Perhaps they would pull at her bag or her hair. He began to jog up the path, taking a fallen branch in his hand to scare away the monkeys. Mrs. Das continued walking, oblivious, trailing grains of puffed rice. Near the top of the incline, before a group of cells fronted by a row of squat stone pillars, Mr. Das was kneeling on the ground, focusing the lens of his camera. The children stood under the arcade, now hiding, now emerging from view.

"Wait for me," Mrs. Das called out. "I'm coming."

Tina jumped up and down. "Here comes Mommy!"

"Great," Mr. Das said without looking up. "Just in time. We'll get Mr. Kapasi to take a picture of the five of us."

Mr. Kapasi quickened his pace, waving his branch so that the monkeys scampered away, distracted, in another direction.

"Where's Bobby?" Mrs. Das asked when she stopped.

Mr. Das looked up from the camera. "I don't know. Ronny, where's Bobby?"

Ronny shrugged. "I thought he was right here."

"Where is he?" Mrs. Das repeated sharply. "What's wrong with all of you?"

They began calling his name, wandering up and down the path a bit. Because they were calling, they did not initially hear the boy's screams. When they found him, a little farther down the path under a tree, he was surrounded by a group of monkeys, over a dozen of them, pulling at his T-shirt with their long black fingers. The puffed rice Mrs. Das had spilled was scattered at his feet, raked over by the monkeys' hands. The boy was silent, his body frozen, swift tears running down his startled face. His bare legs were dusty and red with welts from where one of the monkeys struck him repeatedly with the stick he had given to it earlier.

"Daddy, the monkey's hurting Bobby," Tina said.

Mr. Das wiped his palms on the front of his shorts. In his nervousness he accidentally pressed the shutter on his camera; the whirring noise of the advancing film excited the monkeys, and the one with the stick began to beat Bobby more intently what are we supposed to do? What if they start attacking?"

"Mr. Kapasi," Mrs. Das shrieked, noticing him standing to one side. "Do something, for God's sake, do something!"

Mr. Kapasi took his branch and shooed them away, hissing at the ones that remained, stomping his feet to scare them. The animals retreated slowly, with a measured gait, obedient but unintimidated. Mr. Kapasi gathered Bobby in his arms and brought him back to where his parents and siblings were standing. As he carried him he was tempted to whisper a secret into the boy's ear. But Bobby was stunned, and shivering with fright, his legs bleeding slightly where the stick had broken the skin. When Mr. Kapasi delivered him to his parents, Mr. Das brushed some dirt off the boy's T-shirt and put the visor on him the right way. Mrs. Das reached into her straw bag to find a bandage which she taped over the cut on his knee. Ronny offered his brother a fresh piece of gum. "He's fine. Just a little scared, right, Bobby?" Mr. Das said, patting the top of his head.

"God, let's get out of here," Mrs. Das said. She folded her arms across the strawberry on her chest. "This place gives me the creeps."

"Yeah. Back to the hotel, definitely," Mr. Das agreed.

"Poor Bobby," Mrs. Das said. "Come here a second. Let Mommy fix your hair." Again she reached into her straw bag, this time for her hairbrush, and began to run it around the edges of the translucent visor. When she whipped out the hairbrush, the slip of paper with Mr. Kapasi's address on it flutered away in the wind. No one but Mr. Kapasi noticed. He watched as it rose, carried higher and higher by the breeze, into the trees where the monkeys now sat, solemnly observing the scene below. Mr. Kapasi observed it too, knowing that this was the picture of the Das family he would preserve forever in his mind.

□

NOTES AND GLOSSARY

(I)

THE DIAMOND NECKLACE

(Guy de Maupassant)

Guy de Maupassant (1850-93) is a great French short story writer and novelist. 'Bould de suif' is considered his finest short story and it deals with the Franco-Prussian war. Maupasssant was the disciple of another great French writer, Flaubert. He also formed a part of a group of writers who call themselves 'naturalists'. Naturalists are writers who were part of a literary movement called 'naturalism' in the late 19th and early 20th century. Naturalists believe that the day-to-day life of the middle and lower classes is a subject worthy of serious literary treatment. They therefore provide very accurate details about everyday life and present them without the artificiality of a plot. Maupassant has written six novels, the most famous among them being Une vie (1883), Bel-Ami (1885) and Piere et jean (1888).

Maupassant has hundreds of stories to his credit and these are usually narrated in a simple and direct manner. His stories generally deal with country folk or urban employees and civil servants, among other social groups. His stories also display a touch of pessimism and seem to reflect a sense of the futility of life.

'The Diamond Necklace' is the story of a less-privileged couple, Mathilde and Loisel. Loisel is a clerk in the Department of Education and his wife Mathilde is unhappy about their social position. Loisel manages to obtain an invitation for them to go to a party at the palace of the ministry. Mathilde is reluctant to go as she owns no finery to show off at the party. What follows is an excellent insight into the material objects that symbolize social status and Maupassant underscores the lack of constancy and meaning in objects that determine one's identity in society.

Glossary

Adorned : decorated

Blunder : mistake or error

Abraded : worn out, damaged (due to long use)

Indignant	: angry, offended
Desolated	: feelings of sadness and emptiness on account of not getting what was desired
Distracted dreams	: longings filling the mind, not allowing clear thought
Vestibules	: a space inside the front door of a building
Oriental	: coming from or associated with eastern Asia, especially China or Japan
Tapestry	: a wall-hanging that is usually a large piece of heavy cloth wit a picture sewn on it using coloured threads
Knee breech	: short trousers that fasten just below the knees
Brick-a-brac	: small attractive objects that are not worth very much
Coquettish	: (here) cleverly arranged in order to attract
Tureen	: a large dish with a lid, used for serving soup or vegetables
Trout	: a river fish
Quail	: a bird with a short tail, hunted for food
Seductive	: attractive
Chagrin	: annoyance and disappointment
Disconsolate	: very sad hopeless
Casket	: a small decorated box for jewellery and other valuables
Anteroom	: a lobby or waiting room
Wraps	: a piece of thick cloth that a woman wears around her shoulders
Overwhelmed	: overcome by emotion
Promissory	: a document promising to pay money before a notes particular date
Usurers	: (old-fashioned) money lender
Perspective	: outlook, point of view
Odious	: very unpleasant
Sou by sou	: here, coin by coin
Robust	: very strong and tough
Awry	: crooked or twisted

(II)
THE LAST LEAF
(O. HENRY)

O.Henry, one of the pseudonymous of American writer William Sydney Porter (1862-1910), was born in North Carolina. He had fourteen short stories published under various pseudonyms, but became best known as O. Henry when it was first used for his story 'Whistling Dick's Christmas Stocking' which appeared in December 1899 issue of Mc Clure's Magazine.

O. Henry was adored by his readers for his wit, warm characterization and plot. He gained international recognition in spite of having often to face harsh criticism of contemporary critics. He was considered the American answer to Guy de Maupassant, the renowned French short story writer of the late nineteenths century. Like his French counterpart, O. Henry is credited with defining the short story as a literary art form and both authors are known for their clever twist endings. Such is the fame of O.Henry's surprise endings that they are often referred to as "O. Henry ending".

O. Henry's stories delve deep into human psychology and depict it with remarkable sympathy and understanding. They are also marked by his sensitive perception of human nature, with realistic detail based on his first-hand experiences in Texas and New York and with wry humour about human situations. He is well known for fusing comedy with pathos, and his stories characteristically have surprise endings.

Most of O. Henry's stories deal with contemporary life in early twentieth century. Many are set in New York City but others are set in small towns and other cities. They deal for the most part with ordinary people, clerks, waitresses, policemen. His tales marked with realistic details and wry humour, are based on his first hand experiences of urban living. 'The Gift of the Magi' and 'The Last Leaf' are two of his well-known stories.

This tale deals with the life of artists in 'quaint old Greenwich Village', a little district west of Washington Square. Old Behrman, who could not paint his masterpiece all his life, actually does so to save the life of 'Johnsy' or Joana in bed with pneumonia in cold November only to lose his own through self-sacrifice. The narrative makes use of irony, contrasts and parallels. The tale has a binary structure based on the life-death, painter-artist, mind-body motifs and is made up of two contrasting halves. The first part of the narrative dwells on Johsy's pessimism having given up on life. Her close and caring friend Sue's determination to see Jonsy get well provides sharp contrast between the conflicting attitudes of the two friends to the ravaging disease and illustrates the impact of mind on the body rendering the curative powers of medical science impotent. The pace of the narrative acquires a sense of urgency paralleling the quickening pace of the falling ivy leaves, each leaf serving as a metaphor in Johnsy's mind of every moment of time of her approaching death. Hence, in the second half of the narrative in which Mr. Behrman is introduced, the metaphor of the last leaf not only provides the old man with the idealistic motive fcr painting his masterpiece to save the young patient's life but helps him to transcend from the mediocrity of being a mere painter to the authenticity of becoming a first-rate artist. The central irony of the narrative hinges on the paradox that it is death which engenders life, for whild old Behrman's assertion of life brings about a reversal in Johnsy's world-view from darkness to light, this very belief heroically leads him to his death.

Glossary

Traversing : crossing over

Gables : any triangular architectural section, usually ornamental, as over a door or window

Pewter mugs : mugs made from a grey metal made by mixing tin and lead

Familiar : friendly (name) or (in the context) pet name

Table d'hote : (pron: taal dot) a communal table for all guest at a hotel

Chicory : a widely cultivated plant whose leaves are used in salad and which substitutes for coffee

Bishop sleeves : wide sleeves once worn by women

Congenial : having the same tastes, habits or temperament

Smiting : attacking

Chivalric : polite and kind behaviour exhibited specially by men towards women

Zephyr : a gentle breeze

Pharmacopoeia : a book containing an official list of medicinal drugs together with articles on their preparation and use

Jew's s-harp : a small musical instrument wit a lyre-shaped metal frame that is held between the teeth when played, and a projecting steel tongue that is plucked to produce a soft twanging sound .

Twang : speech sound produce through the nose and mouth

Clock sleeves : an embroidered or woven decoration on the side of the stocking or sock

Ragtime : a style of jazz music

Idaho : one of the rock mountain states in the U.S.A.

Solicitously : with concern

Gnarled : twisted

Broth : a thin clear soup of meat, fish or vegetables

Satyr : (pron: sat-er) a Greek god with a man's body and a goats' legs and horns.

Mistress's robe : here a reference to the art of painting (art form personified)

Daub : a small amount (of paint) spread carelessly

Mastiff-in-waiting : waiting to serve like a large strong dog

Juniper : any of various evergreen coniferous trees or shrubs having spine-tipped needles

Easel : a frame, usually in the form of an upright tripod upon which something may be displayed or which may support an artist's canvas

Flibbertigibit : (pron: flibertijibit) a silly scatterbrained person, especially a young girl

Livelong : long or seemingly long in passing

Serrated : having tooth-like projections (like a saw)

Dissolution : disintegration

Eaves : the projecting edge of the roof

Janitor : caretaker

Palette : a board, typically with a hole for the thumb, upon which as artist mixes colours.

(III)

A cup of Tea

(Katherine Mansfield)

Katherine Mansfield (1888-1923) was the pen name of Kathleen Mansfield Beauchamp. She was born in Wellington, New Zealand and was educated at Queens College in London. She was a master of short stories and was a talented cellist too. Katherine Mansfield's first published stories were in the High School Reporter, the Wellington Girl's High school magazine, I 1898 and 1899. She continued to write until her untimely death at the age of thirty-five, due to tuberculosis. Three volumes of her stories appeared during her lifetime,. Mansfield's Work has been translated into 26 languages, and in 1988, the centennial of her birth, five international conferences focused on her life and work. In addition to her stories, the letters and journals published by her husband, John Middleton Murry, reveal intimate details of her life and thoughts.

Her stories communicate to the reader through small and fleeting experiences in life. She writes in a simple and uncomplicated style. Katherine Mansfield belongs to a 'new dawn' in English literature alongside T.S. Eliot, James Joyce and Virginia Woolf. Katherine Mansfield's stories are innovative in many ways. The plot of her stories feature simple things like a doll's house.

Rosemary Fell lived at a town near Paris in France. She was an ordinary-looking, "young brilliant, extremely modern, exquisitely well-dressed" and culturally up-to-date lady. She had been married two years and had a darling boy named Michael. Her husband paid her much more than due attention. They were so rich that the lady, instead of shopping in the local markets, used to go to Paris for the purpose and collect from there the choicest of things that would satisfy her most. Even the shopkeepers knew her habits of buying most fashionable and costly things and used to flatter her in a characteristically cajoling manner. For instance, a particular shopkeeper in Curzon Street always used to flatter her by saying that he preserved certain costly and fashionable items exclusively for her, for she was his only customer who could appreciate the value of such things.

One winter afternoon she visited his shop. The shopkeeper exhibited to her 'an exquisite little enamel box with a glaze so fine it looked as though it had been baked in cream'. Rosemary examined the box, liked it very much and loved it. But the price of the box was twenty-eight guineas. After hearing about the price of the box she decided not to buy it right then but asked the shopkeeper to keep it for her.

Rosemary then came out of the shop. It was raining. The atmosphere outside was dark and gloomy, with the newly lit lamps burning dimly. "People hurried by, hidden under their hateful umbrellas." Rosemary thought of going back home and having "an extra-special tea". But the very moment she thought it, her eyes fell on "a young girl, thin, dark, shadowy" and she heard a voice 'like a sigh, almost like a sob', addressing her, "Madam, may I speak to you for a moment?" The young girl looked like 'a little battered creature, with enormous eyes'. She was of Rosemary's age. She 'clutched at her coat-collar with reddened hands, and shivered as though she had just come out of the water". "Would you let me have the price of a cup of tea?" She stammered. But she did not sound like a beggar. There was something simple sincere in her voice. Rosemary was surprised.

She asked the young girl, "Then have you no money at all?" "None, Madam", came the answer. Rosemary thought it 'more than extraordinary'. The situation seemed to give her the opportunity of an adventure, the like of which she had read in the novels of Dostoevsky or seen in plays on the stage. She thought of taking the girl home and the thought thrilled her. She imagined how her friends would be amazed when they would know it from her. She ultimately offered to take the girl home to tea with her. The girl reacted strangely to rosemary's proposal. She drew back startled and even stopped trembling for a moment. Rosemary tried to make her feel easy by touching her arm and saying to her smilingly "I mean it." The young girl refused to believe Rosemary. Rosemary repeatedly entreated the girl to come along with her. But the girl grew suspicious of Rosemary and thought the later was actually trying to take her to the police station. Rosemary assured her that she only wanted the girl to feel warm and to hear whatever she would care to tell her. But the girl was hungry and the "hungry people are easily led". So, she agreed to go with Rosemary who then had 'a feeling of triumph'. "She was going to prove to this girl that wonderful things did happen in life, that fairy godmothers were real, that rich people had hearts, and that women were sisters."

However, Rosemary reached her home along with the young girl by her car. It was a large luxurious house, with separate rooms for each member of the family. Rosemary took the girl to her own room to make her feel comfortable and to save her from being started at by the servants. She wanted 'to be natural' in her treatment towards the girl. She asked the girl to sit down in the comfortable chair in her own bedroom. But the girl looked dazed, afraid and 'rather stupid'. She stayed standing just inside the door 'with her hands by her sides and her mouth slightly open'. Rosemary bade the girl take off her hat and coat. The girl, unable to wait any longer, said to Rosemary lightly and strangely: "I'm very sorry madam, but I'm going to faint. I shall go off, madam, if I don't have something" for food. Rosemary, jolted into an awareness of the girl's dire need for something for food, immediately ordered for tea and some brandy, when the girl almost cried out, "No, I don't want brandy. I never drink brandy. It's a cup of tea I want, madam," and she burst into tears. Rosemary tried to soothe and contort her so much so that the girl 'forgot to be shy' and 'forgot everything except that they were both women'. The tea came. The girl was served the tea and 'a slight meal' of 'sandwiches' and 'bread and butter'. The effect of this was marvelous. It refreshed and replenished the girl. Rosemary, who neither drank nor ate anything but smoked, lit a fresh cigarette and began to wait for the girl to begin her story. "And when did you have your last meal?" She asked softly.

But, at that moment, Rosemary's husband, Philip, came in. the girl revealed her name. She was Miss Smith. She now looked 'strangely still and unafraid.' Philip stared at Miss Smith so long that Rosemary did not like it and wanted to have 'a little talk' with him. Rosemary and her husband went out of the room together. Philip enquired who the girl was and why actually Rosemary had brought her home. Rosemary explained the whole thing. "But what on earth are you going to do with her?" Cried Philip to whom Rosemary answered quickly, "Be nice to her. Be frightfully nice to her. Look after her." Philip said that it was impossible and absurd. Rosemary eagerly persuaded him to be nice to Miss Smith just for pleasing her by honoring her desire if not for anything else. But a remarkable change came over Rosemary, although she was clever enough to hide this change , when Philip began to praise the beauty of Miss Smith by saying, "She is so astonishingly pretty...she's absolutely lovely...I was bowled over when I came into your room just now." Rosemary, soon after hearing these words, went out of the library, but not back to her bedroom. She went to her writing room and sat down at her desk and began to repeatedly remember the superlative adjectives and expressions with which her husband praised the beauty of Miss Smith. His panegyric of Smith's beauty pained Rosemary. She opened a drawer and took out three one-pound notes and holding them squeezed in her hand went back to her bedroom where she had left Miss Smith. She went back to her husband who was still in the library, half an hour later, to tell him that Miss Smith had left the house, and that she 'could not keep her against her will'.

Rosemary then beautified herself by doing her hair, darkening her eyes a little and putting on her pearl. She went close to Philip, put up her hands and touched his cheeks and said in a touching, sweet husky tone, and "Do you like me?" "I like you awfully", he said, and he held her tighter. "Kiss me", she said. Then there was a pause. Rosemary said dreamily, "I saw a fascinating little box today. It costs twenty-eight guineas May I have it?" Philip endearingly gave his consent to her buying that box. But that was not nor really what Rosemary wanted to say. "Philip", she whispered, and she pressed her head against his bosom, "am I pretty?"

Glossary

Quaint : unusual and attractive esp. in a an old-fashioned way

Stumpy : stumpy legs and fingers are short and thick in an unattractive way

Cavern : a large cave

Battered : battered women children etc. Women or children who have been violently treated by their husband or fathers.

(IV)
The Lost Child

(Mulk Raj Anand)

Indian novelist, short-story writer, and art critic writing in English. Mulk Raj Anand was among the first writers to render Punjabi and Hindustani idioms into English. Called the Zola or Blazae of India, Anand drew a realistic and sympathetic portrait of the poor of his country. With Raja Rao and R.K. Narayan, he has been regarded as one the "founding fathers" of the Indian English novel.

"And he had soon become possessed with an overwhelming desire to live their life. He had been told they were sahibs, superior people. He had felt that to put on their clothes made one sahib too. So he tried to copy them as well as he could in the exigencies of his peculiarly Indian circumstances."

Mulk Raj Anand was born in Peshawar, as the son of Lal Chand, a coppersmith and soldier, and Ishwant Kaur. Anand rebelled early on against his father's subservience to the British authorities. His first texts were born as a reaction to the trauma of the suicide of an aunt, who had been excommunicated for dining with a Muslim woman. An unhappy love for a Muslim girl, who was married, inspired some of his poetry. Anand attended Khalsa College, Amritsar, and entered the University of Punjab in 1921, graduating with honors in 1924. Thereafter Anand did his additional studies at Cambridge and at London University, receiving his Ph.D. in 1929. He studied-and later lectured-at League of Nations School of Intellectual Cooperation in Geneva. Between 1932 and 1945 Anand lectured, on and off, at Workers Educational Association in London.

'The Lost Child', which Anand wrote in London in 1929, put him on the world's literary map. As the story opens one beholds running between his parents legs a boy of six on the way to a fair Anand calls it "the festival of spring". In the tradition of a folk tale, the story begins with a fair scene in a village. The happy breeze blowing in the village during the spring has been pictured as:

"It was the festival of spring. From the wintry shades of narrow lanes and alleys emerged a gaily clad humanity. Thick as a swarm of bright - coloured, rabbits issuing from a warren. They entered the flooded sea of sparking silver sunshine outside the city gates and sped towards the fair. Some walked, some rode on horses, other sat, being carried in bamboo and bullock carts. One little boy ran between his parent's legs, brimming over with life and laughter. The joyous morning gave greetings and unashamed invitations to all to come away into the fields, full of flowers and songs."

The child is drawn towards the dancing dragon flies, the

multicolored blossoms to all that the beautiful "world of eye and ear" has to offer him. At the fair itself, the child is fascinated by the things around him and he starts an unending chorus of "I want". At one moment he wants burfi, at another, a multicolored balloon, and at yet another, a garland of gulmohar though only to draw a blank from his parents. He is particularly fascinated by the ferric wheel and is keen to have a joy-ride on it. He stands raptly before for a long time before bursting forth: "I want to go on the round about please, father mother". But his parents are not there to answer him this time. The child finds himself lost:

"A full, deep cry rose within his dry throat and with a sudden jerk of his body he ran from where he stood, crying in red fear, "mother, father! Tears rolled down his eyes, hot and fierce; his flushed face was convulsed with fear. Panic - stricken, he ran to one side first, then to the other hither, thither and in all directions, knowing not where to go. "Mother, father! He wailed! With a moist, shrill breath now, his throat being wet with swallowing his spittle. His yellow turban came untied and his clothes wet with perspiration, became muddy where the dust had mixed with the sweat of his body. His light frame seemed heavy as a mass of lead."

By ending the story thus Anand brings the reader face to face with the bitterness of reality. The child's loss in the fair reminds him of his own, in the world fair. Like the youngster, he too is drawn to the world's attractions and craves for all types of things. His desire for worldly things, however, lasts as long as he has a sense of security. The moment it is withdrawn he becomes aware of his human predicament, of his isolation in the world that is callous, strong and indifferent. It is this inhuman world that the child encounters while searching for his lost parents:

"Every little inch of space here was congested with men but he ran through peoples legs, his little sob lingering: 'Mother, Father !', Near the entrance to the temple, however, the crowd become very thick: men jostled each other, heavy men, with flashing, murderous eyes and hefty shoulders, the poor child struggled to thrust a way between their feet but, knocked to and fro by their brutal movements, he might have been trampled underfoot had he not shrieked at the highest, pitch of his voice: Father, Mother!"

Anand's greatness here lies in giving his childhood traumatic experience, a universal significance. By not revealing the name of the child, his parents and the shrine the writer has made them impersonal, representative figures. The unnamed child steps out of the framework of the story and lives in timeless humanity, thus attaining fabulous character and resembling the character of a folk tale. Through the child's feeling of getting lost in the story he reveals the eternal varieties of human existence. Much in the fashion of the famous psychologists Anand places the sense of security on top of the hierarchy of one's basic needs. As this sense of security is the natural corollary of 'kin - bonds', particularly, the parent - child relationship, its loss inevitably leads to dread of isolation, frustration, even to neurosis. Here Anand seems to be maintaining that an individual feels powerless, insecure and isolated when the sense of securities offered by primary ties are withdrawn and he becomes aware of himself as a separate identity. The story may well illustrate the modern man's sense of isolation in the face of a hostile, insecure world.

A man from the crowd tries to quiet him. He even offers to buy him a toy, garments and sweets and he wants to take him on a joy ride. The child, however, will have nothing to do with him. He keeps repeating:

"I want my father, I want my mother"

The story may be viewed as an allegory of the loss of the paradisiacal innocence of man. The child may be taken to represent human consciousness in the early stages of purity and innocence. It is only when he comes in contact with reality that he becomes really susceptible to experience. And experience is not always pleasant or wholesome. His separation from his parents may imply fall from grace and banishment from Eden.

"The story veers round the less of paradisiacal state of man....His separation from his parents implies fall from grace and banishment from Eden. He strays into the hell of his own making because he cannot resist temptations. His fall like Adam's is the result of his inordinate cravings and desires, the fact that he renounces the once cherished pleasures gives promise of return to grace."

'The lost child' is complete as a work of art. Anand rightly calls it a "prose poem," for it emanates from a basis poetic impulse - the song of innocence and experience in the mind of man. An exploration of child psychology, the story takes us in the presence of illumination, mapping out new dimensions of reality. But most of all, the power of orchestrating different themes and motives into a fused harmony gives it its incomparable excellence:

"A shower of young flowers fell upon the child as he entered the grove, and forgetting his parents, he began to gather in the raining petals in his hands. But lo! he heard the cooing of the doves and ran towards his parents, shouting: The Dove! The Dove! The raining petals dropped from his forgotten hands. A curious look was in his parents' faces till a koel struck out a note of love and released their pent - up - souls."

Glossary

Warren : the underground home of rabbits

Pout : to push out your lips because you are

	annoyed or to look sexually attractive
Saturate	: to mix
Prance	: to walk in an energetic way
Chaperon	: an older woman in former times who went out with a young unmarried woman on social occasions and was responsible for her behaviour
Convulse	: if a part of your body convulses, it moves violently and you are not able to control it.
Importunate	: always asking for things in an annoying or unreasonable way

(V)

The Barber's Trade Union

(Mulk Raj Anand)

The title story of 'Barber's Trade Union' very well illustrates Anand's insistence on the dignity of man, irrespective of caste, class and profession. Like Bakha in untouchable, Chandu is an outcaste, subjected to the contempt and tyranny of the high-caste Hindus. But this very tyranny awakens him to an awareness of his miserable existence. When the crisis comes, he accepts the challenges and succeeds in making his oppressors realize that they can no longer deprive him of his right to lead an honorable life.

Chandu, the barber boy, blazes a new trail for his profession, the interest lying in the manner in which he achieves his rare feat, thus moving from sterile existence to a new kind of freedom.

On his occasional visit to the neighboring town, he develops new-fangled ideas about his trade. Dressed in white turban, white tunic, and pumps, he carries a leather bag in the manner of the town physician. One day I was thrilled to find Chandu at the door of my house in the morning. He was dressed up in a white turban, a white rubber coat (a little too big for him but nevertheless very splendid), a pair of pumps in which I could see my face reflected in clear silhouette, and he had a leather bag in his hand. He was setting off on his round and had come to show me how grand he looked in his new rig - out. "Marvellous! I said, 'Marvelous!"

In this new garb, he goes on his daily round of shaving. He is snubbed by the village landlord and by the moneylender for wearing funny clothes and for being avant-garde.

"'Ram! Ram! Ram!' said Bijay Chand, the burly landlord, touching the sacred thread which hung over his ear since he had just been to the lavatory. 'The son of a pig ! He is bringing a leather bag of cow-hide into our house and a coat of the marrow of, I don't know, some other animal, and those evil black Angrezi shoes. Get out! Get out! You son of a devil! You will defile my religion. I suppose you have no fear of anyone now that your father is dead!"

"Go away you, swine, go away and wear clothes befitting your low status as a barber, and don't let me see you practicing any of your new-fangled notions, or else I will have you flogged!"

Moved by the overbearing ness of humiliation and abuse, Chandu revolts against the situation. He retaliates by refusing to shave them in future. He henceforth does all his shaving business in the town. In the meantime, the elders of the village must go without being shaved, their unkempt and shabby looks provoking amusement in the village. Chandu enjoys the fun most of all and has the last laugh. The zamindar for the most suffers the revolt by Chandu as he is threatened by his wife:

"And it was said that at least the landlord's wife threatened to run away with somebody, because, being younger than her husband by twenty years, she had borne with him as long as he kept himself in trim, but was now disgusted with him beyond the limits of reconciliation."

Later, he organizes a trade union against Zamindar Vijay Chand to teach him a lesson for his land lordism and tyranny. The story depicting the life of common weaker section of India united against the exploiters is widespread and universal in character. The story's centre of gravity lies in the characterization of Chandu. He is sprightly, resourceful, and witty; it is no wonder that he is held in high esteem by the child narrator. Chandu is an ardent advocate of the new order of things. He stands firmly against caste, custom, and convention, and when the occasion arises, he pays back the tyrannical village elders in their own coin. He is sincere as well as advanced in his profession, and therefore he wins admiration for his craft.

As for the technique employed by the author, the first person narration serves the twofold purpose of dramatizing the incidents from a distance and of throwing the hero's character into sharp relief. The comic method may seem at variance with the serious intention, but it actually helps Top intensity the total effect. The beginning of the story is mock - heroic:

"Among the makers of modern India. Chandu, the barber boy of our village, has a place, which will be denied to him unless I press for the recognition of his contribution to history. Chandu's peculiar claim to recognition rested, to tell the truth, on an exploit of which he did not know the full significance. But, then, unlike most great men of India today, he had no very exaggerated notion of his own importance, though he shared with them a certain na_ve egotism which was sometimes rather charming.

The mock-heroic vein continues throughout the story. When the village landlord sees chandu in a new rig, he bursts into torrents of speech, the effect of which is almost ludicrous!

"The son of a pig! He is bringing a leather bag of cowhide into our house and a coat of the marrow of, I don't know, some other animal, and those evil black Angrezi boots, Get out! Get out! You will defile my religion. I suppose you have no fear of anyone."

The scene in which the village elders are exposed to ridicule in the presence of a congregation of peasants is a masterpiece of comic construction:

"Ha! Ha!" I shouted hilariously, struck by the contradiction of the big thick moustache (which I knew the landlord dyed) with the prickly white bush on his jowls. "Ha! Ha!" I roared, "a sick lion! He looks seedy."

"Sh!" warned Chandu, "Don't make a row! But look at the Sahukar. He looks like a leper with the brown tinge of tobacco on his walrus moustache which I once used to trim. Now you run past the shop and call "Beavers, Beavers. They can't say anything to you!" I was too impetuous a disciple of the impish Chandu to wait to deliberate. "Beavers ! Beavers !" I shouted."

Anand has amply demonstrated his mastery of the grotesque. The description of the shabby appearance of the elders and the mirth it provokes in an instance in point:

"The rumour about the barber boy's strike spread, and jokes about the unkempt beards of the elders of the village became current in every home. Even those who were of high castes, even the members of high castes, even the members of the families of elders, began to giggle with laughter at the shabby appearance of the great ones and made rude remarks about their persons."

In fact, irony is central to Anand's method, which unites the two opposite poles of levity and seriousness. The story is a fine example of the ironic treatment of a fairly serious theme.

The story is marked by it species and compact structure. This story intends to put up an intense and serious message in a small scale. Instead of its fabulous character and intense message carrying a serious theme in a light mood, it is legendry in nature. The way Anand has mixed the flavour of modernism in the character of Chandu is really notable. The story illustrates a contrasting reaction to modernity. Chandu the enterprising (a character with both head and heart) but rustic barber boy who is bitten by the bug of modernity dares wear the clothes of a doctor and is threatened with dire consequences for this act of impudence by the village elders. In the end it is chandu who wins, when he goes on a strike, organizes a union and is successful in breaking the age - old customs of the barber's dancing attendance on the village elders. In his apparently simple story Anand weaves a network of traditional and modern beliefs and exploits fully the folk imagination and modern sense of equality.

Glossary

Exploit	: Great achievement
Wallowed	: to allow yourself to relish utterly
Condescended	: to regard oneself better than other
Emoluments	: additional incentive given in addition to salary
Strutted	: to walk in a proud way trying to look important
Cantankerous	: arguing and complaining
Sheen	: lustre
Precariously	: in a way that is likely to fall or damaged
Impish	: very evil
Giggle	: to laugh

(VI)

A Horse and Two Goats

(R. K. Narayan)

R.K. Narayan (1906-2001), one of the best-loved novelists and short story writers, was born in Chennai (Madras) and was educated in Mysore, Karnataka. After graduating, he took to writing as a profession. Graham Greene, the English novelist, appreciated Narayan's works and persuaded some publishers to bring out his novels. In 1956, he was invited by the Rockfeller Foundation to visit America. He recorded the impressions of his visit in his book My Dateless Dairy. The portrait of Mahatma Gandhi in his book Waiting for the Mahatma was well received by American readers. Viking Press published his novel the Guide in 1958.This famous novel won the Sahitya Akademi award and was made into a film in English and Hindi by Vijay Anand. Several American and British universities honoured him. The University of Mysore, the Delhi University and the University of Leeds conferred honorary doctorates on him. In 1989, he was nominated to the Rajya Sabha. The Indian Government honored him with the Padma Bhushan in 1964 and Padma Vibhushan in 2000.

Swami and Friends, The Dark Room, The English Teacher, The Bachelor of Arts, Waiting for the Mahatma, The Man-Eater of Malgudi, The Financial expert, The Guide, Gods, Demons and others, The Vendor of Sweets, Talkative Man and Mr Sampath are some of his famous works. Commenting on R K Narayan's stories, the American novelist John Updike says, 'Few writers since Dickens can match the effect of colourful teeming that Narayan's fictional town of Malgudi conveys; its population is sharply chiseled as a temple frieze, and as endless, with always, one feels, more characters around the corner.' Narayan's style is an exquisite blend of keen observation and realism, gentle humour, pathos and subtle irony, lucidity and elegance.

In this short story R.K.Narayan is at his brilliant best as he exploits the full comic potential of the East-West binaries in terms of country, race, culture, religion, economic status and most important of all, language. The chance encounter between a rich American businessman from New York visiting India for the first time and Muni, an old half-starved and impoverished Tamillian herdsman from Kritam, probably the tiniest village in India, leads to an exchange in which their conversation in their respective mother tongue is almost comparable to a conversation between two deaf men! Their 'basis of understanding' could not have been more imperfect as neither knows the other one's language.

Turned out by his wife for failing to provide for even one full meal, Muni sets off to graze his two miserable goats which were too skinny for anyone to even want to buy them. He sorely wished to be rid of them. Having sat the whole day on the pedestal of a nearly life-sized clay statue of a prancing horse with a mustachioed warrior standing beside it, Muni observes a station-wagon driven by a khaki-clad red-faced foreigner splutter to a stop in front of him. Suspecting him to be a policeman, Muni's first instinct is to run from the stranger when the latter accosts him in English. Muni's knowledge of English vocabulary was limited to the words "yes, no." But the foreigner's friendly gesture in offering the old man a cigarette gradually puts him at ease. What follows is an easy flow of a parallel conversation with neither of them realizing that they are talking at cross purposes. The American is taken up with the statue of the horse and mistaking Muni to be its owner, thrusts a hundred-rupee note as its purchase price. As the American pats the goats in a genial manner, Muni in turn mistakes this action to be an offer for his goats. His dreams having been finally realized Muni hurries home with the money to his wife leaving his goats behind with the red man. Stopping a passing truck, the American is helped by a couple of men to load the horse into his vehicle. The comic irony in the contrast and the incongruity of the two different worlds is sustained and deepened as the narrative is led to an anti-climax when the puzzled Muni discovers that instead of being carried off by the American, his goats have returned home to him!

Glossary

Furrowed : formed grooves

Gargoyle : a rainwater drainage spout in the form of a

	grotesque animal or human figure
Balustrade	: decorative railing
Sallied	: set out
Pedestal	: base or support for a statue or column
Crook	: a curved or hooked tool
Faggots	: a bundle of sticks
Drumstick	: the fruit of a pod-bearing leguminous plant (Indian: 'Suanjana ki phali')
Coriander	: Indian 'dhania'
Gingelley oil	: Indian 'til ka tael'
Imp	: a small, mischievous imaginary being
Itinerant	: travelling on job
Impelled	: forced to do
Castor oil	: Indian 'undi ka tael'
Recoup	: recover
Cronies	: old friends of long standing
Lounging	: lying or sitting lazily
Affluence	: prosperity
Gawky	: awkward and clumsy
Fancied	: wished for something
Elated	: made happy
Pestilence	: epidemic of a disease
Afflicted	: caused distress
Scraggy	: skinny
Progeny	: offspring
Barren	: unable to have children
Meandered	: wandered aimlessly
Prancing	: jump forward on back legs
Scythe-like	: like a long curved single-edged blade
Aquiline	: thin, curved and pointed
Vandal	: somebody who damages property
Lantana	: tropical shrub with brightly coloured spikes of yellow or orange flowers
Scrounge	: get from any available source
Extricate	: free with difficulty
Gainsay	: deny
Courtesy	: polite or considerate behaviour
Took stock	: made an estimate of
Wary	: cautious
Detractors	: adverse critics
Ingratiatingly	: in a manner to please in order to seek

	favours
Implored	: requested earnestly
Sidled	: moved sideways
Driftwood	: broken floating wood
Get a kick	: (informal use) to feel a thrill
Parangi	: 'firangi', foreign
Quip	: a short, clever remark
Predicament	: difficult situation
Discoursed	: sermonized
Bearish trend	: anticipating a fall in price (stock exchange)
Famished	: extremely hungry
Clump	: cluster of things
Thicket	: thick growth of bushes
Siphoned off	: to remove by means of a bent tube (a siphone)

(VII)
SELVI
(R.K. Narayan)

Readers accustomed to R. K. Narayan's gentle comic irony and tongue-in-cheek style will find this story to be serious and somber in tone but with an irony that is lacking in humour. Selvi is a portrayal of a gifted singer whose talent is carefully nurtured, groomed and exploited commercially for over two decades by Mohan who claims to be her husband. Having been a former Gandhian, Mohan makes subtle use of cosmetics for touching up her face as he did not want any one to suspect that he encouraged modern artificial aids to heighten his wife's personality. Through sheer perseverance, financial expertise and careful monitoring of her publicity and physical appearance he builds up her image to the status of a much sought-after celebrity. She is admired and revered almost as a goddess. But Mohan always makes sure to keep all and sundry at a distance except for a select few, specially those in position of power who are allowed to meet her, though always so in his presence.

The central irony of the story is located in the suppression of Selvi's private voice at the expense of her public 'singing' voice. Jealously guarded and imprisoned in 'a fortress of invisible wall', she never deviates from the text scripted by Mohan. She is gently and unobtrusively isolated from her mother, brother and sister as her public engagements increase. The eclipsing of her private identity by the carefully and artificially cultivated public one reduces her to a state of benumbed indifference. But the acute sense of loss at the death of her mother who had taught her music and had been her guru, prompts her for the first time to take an independent decision to live in her mother's humble home instead of the huge residence of Sir Frederick Lawley bought for her by Mohan with her money. It is then that she finds her 'true' voice as she sings freely to a swelling gathering from the neighbourhood, day after day without any charge. When repeated efforts to meet Selvi privately fail to materialize, Mohan attempts to meet her alone at home at night. In refusing firmly to meet him at the inappropriate hour of the night, Selvi is finally able to assert her own true identity.

Glossary

Ethereal : heavenly, spirit-like
Flourished : grew thickly
Confounding : puzzling
Speculation : gossip
Habitu : (pron: ha-bichoo-ay) a regular visitor of a place
Confinement : imprisonment
Ceremoniously : formally and conventionally
Assiduous : constant or untiring in application
Exorbitant : excessive
Remuneration : pay, reward
Conjure : to cause to be or become by magic
Stenographer : a shorthand typist
Assortment : variety
Blasphemous : contemptuous of sacred things
Gigantic : (pron: jai-gan-tik) huge
Oblivious : absent-mindedly unaware
Toiletry : any article, preparation or cosmetic used in washing and dressing oneself
Vouchsafed : condescended to accept
Versatility : many-sided ability
Riveted : fixed (attention)
Proximity : immediate nearness
Calibre : capacity or character
Interpose : to put in by way of interruption
Unobtrusively : without thrusting forward; unnoticeably
Isolate : detach, seclude
Automation : machine-like
Nondescript : not distinctive enough to be described

Script : the actor's, director's written copy of the text of a play, film
Frenzy : a state of violent excitement
Citadel : a fortress
Impregnable : that cannot be taken by force
Frittering : squandering, wasting
Thronged : crowded

(VIII)
HEAR ME SANJAYA...
(Shashi Deshpande)

Shashi Deshpande (b. 1938) is an award-winning Indian novelist and short story writer. She was born in Karnataka, southern India, the daughter of a renowned Sanskrit scholar and dramatist, Shriranga. She was educated in Mumbai and Bangalore and obtained degrees in economics, law and English literature. She started her career as a short story writer and went on to write novels, children's books and essays as well. She was awarded the Sahitya Akademi (National Academy of Letters) award in 1990. Her publications include the Dark Holds No Terrors (1980), that Long Silence (1988), A Matter of Time (1996), The Bindin Vine (2002), and writing from the Margin and other Essays (2003). Shashi Deshpande writes about the unspoken realities of women's lives, drawing attention to issues ranging from loneliness and rejection within arranged marriages, strained relationships between mothers and daughters, husbands and wives among the middle classes, and other issues affecting women. Through her writing, Deshpande has empowered and given voice to the silent women who are shackled by tradition.

Deshpande usually has the heroine as the narrator, and employs a kind of stream-of-consciousness technique. The narrative goes back and forth in time, so the narrator can describe events with the benefit of hindsight. It would not be correct to term her a feminist, because there is nothing doctrinaire about her fiction; she simply portrays, in depth, the meaning of being a woman in modern India. Exemplary of her worldview is A Matter of Time, her first novel published in the United States: it is the tale of a woman abandoned by a man. The woman is Sumi, who has three daughters; the man is her husband, a professor named Gopal; and her abandonment forces her to return to the family's home in Bangalore. The issues Sumi faces are not Indian problems; they are universal ones - not just the difficulties in her marriage, but the conflicts within her family as well.

Shashi Deshpande is a best selling novelist and well known short story writer .She occupies a place of eminence among Indian women writers writing in English. “Here me, Sanjay ...” is a moving and confessional tale of Kunti, the mother-figure of the Indian epic 'Mahabharata'. Culled from Shashi Deshpande's second volume of her collected stories, it belongs to the early periods (the seventies and eighties) of the writer's creative works .During this period, as Deshpande herself avers, she found herself exploring the Puranas and the epics more and more in her attempt to reject all that had been said, written and told to her. In these stories based on the epical characters and situations Deshpande adds a new dimension by discarding images, stereotypes, requisitioning myths and starting afresh ,crawling into the minds of her characters and painting their inner landscape.

Sanjaya, according to mythology, was the charioteer of the blind king Dhritarasthta in the 'Mahabharata' known for his truthfulness, Sanjaya was the king's window to the outside world. This accurate and truthful reporting of the Great War between the Kauravas and the Pandavas won him great favour and respect and when the story begins, he like a loyal and faithful companion of the king accompanies him to the forest along with Gandhari and Kunti. Kunti's outpourings to Sanjaya forms the subject matter of this beautiful tale sensitively rendered by Shashi Deshpande. What strikes the readers most is that the narrator has given an altogether new and different interpretation of action of women characters of the great epic, particularly that of Kunti .at the outset kunti expresses her satisfaction at Gandhari's decision to remove herself imposed negation of vision and comments as to how it had brought comfort and removed the sense of guilt from her husband Dhristargshta . Kunti is haunted by the voices of the two queens, her mothers-in-law who hardly spoke in the palace and strongly feels that Bhishma had erred in taking the vow of celibacy. Perhaps, this could have avoided the great war .Kunti further reveals to Sanjaya about her relationship with her husband, Pandu, her jealousy towards the latter's second wife, the beautiful Madri who entrusted hers sons Nakula and Sahadeva to her care .She also laments having imposed her decision on the impetuous and pampered Dravapadi to be the common wife her five sons when the latter could have been happy and contented as Arjuna's wife. Kunti also reminisces about her dropping of the name 'Pritha' used by her maid in order to cover up the birth of her son Karan prior to her wedlock. Kunti further reveals her pathos at Karan's refusal to accept her as his mother she also comments on Draupadi's strained relationship with Subhadhra Arjun second wife and mother of Abhimanyu, and how her jelings softened after the tragic and untimely death of the young warrior. Apart from Kunti's confusions, the story also highlights the ultimate truth that the protagonist gains regarding the futility of war and the meaninglessness of the so called brave actions and achievements of the victors. She is all sympathy for her sons who lost their sons in the war, for Dhritarashta and Gandhari who are haunted every night in their dreams by the memories of their dead sons, the Kauroves in this extremely mournful tale, Shashi Deshpande leads us to the same cathartic effect as experienced by her protagonist, Kunit. 'Hear me, Sanjaya...' is a singular example of a story where the narrator has succeeded in her mission of rewriting reasoning and recreating new tales from the corpus of old of the Puranas and the epics of India.

Glossary

Drudgery : hard boring work

Endearment : an action or word that expresses your love for someone.

Pamper : to look after some one too kindly or very kindly.

(IX)

STEEL HAWK

(Bhabani Bhattacharya)

Bhabani Bhattacharya (1906-1988) was one of the foremost Indian fiction writers who consciously chose English as his medium of expression. He was determined to present the Indian experience in its distinctive and characteristic forms more rural than urban. He shaped himself as a purposive writer and a novelist of ideas rather than a mere congenital novelist Interested in depicting life as a receptacle Bhattacharya courageously chose the major problems of Indian socio cultural transformation. He himself asserts that Art must teach-Art must, breach. Bhabani Bhattacharya holds that 'a' novel must have a social purpose- purposeless an and literature which is in vogue does not appear to me a sound judgment.

Like most novelists Bhattacharya wrote stories also but he does not seem to have taken much interest in the form. Dorothy Shimer Calls his stories 'Slight Stories' and says that 'short shorts' are essentially character sketches: He is indubitable 'a reasoned master of the short story form. Dorothy.

Shimer has before her mind short story writers who Chekhov Katherine Mansfield Somerset Maugham O' Henry' and so on and naturally funds Bhattacharya wanting as a short story writer. But when we liken him to R.K. Narayan Raja Rao, and Mulk Raj Anand, we find that he has the capacity to turn out good stories like them but the fact is that he hasn't written enough number of stories to help us say some thing decisive about him as a story writer. The only collection of short stories 'steel hawk and other stories was published in Delhi in 1968.

The last story in this is 'Steel Hawk', which is the tale of a village cartman who goes to see a 'flying wonder', an aero plane, which has landed a few miles away from the village. On the way he gives lift to Kamini, a school teacher's wife, and her six-year old daughter, Babla. As the cart runs, he tells the story of his grandmother who saw, when she was 14 or 15, a train for the first time, 'big and quiet as an elephant'. The grandma had said, "To see this I must have earned merit by a hundred and one good deeds!" Bishen, the cartman, is sorry that his grandma is too old and too week and crazy to go with him. When he sets eyes on the aircraft, which is a helicopter, he is disappointed, though in his fancy he rides, with his grandma, the steel-hawk and goes zooming into the sky. The tale is a simple attempt to depict the peasant imagination and, as Dorothy Shimer points out, it' doesn't come off'. Probably Bhattacharya's talent for humour does not have in it the astringency of wit, because of which his humour tends to be simplistic.

Glossary

Thwack : to hit someone or something moving a short loved sound.

Lithe : Having a body that moves easily and gracefully

Trek : to make a long and difficult journey, esp. on foot

Close-cropped : a close cropped grass or hair is cut very short

With bated breath : feeling very conscious or excited

Wag : to shake your finger or head repeatedly, esp. to show disapproval

Splutter : to make short sharp noise, like someone spitting.

Hump : a large round shape that rises above the surface of the ground or surface.

Flank : the side of an animals or person's body, between the riles and the hips.

(X)
THE THIEF

(Ruskin Bond)

Ruskin Bond is one of the most prolific and leading short-story writers in Indian English. He deserves to be recognized as a unique writer who explored India and its various aspects in a manner of his own, and that has provided a niche for him in literature today.

Ruskin Bond's thematic preoccupations, characterization, plot construction, nativization of the form of short story and style successfully act as a vehicle of articulating his vision of the world in his short stories.

Bond's stories delve deep into human psyche and unfurl human mind in relation to nature and environment. The incidents and situation depicted in his stories are not wholly fictional. He projects a part of his personality into his stories to make them authentic and interesting. He is not content to describe the things as they happened. He probes deep into how they happened and why they happened. He examines his characters from the inside and analyses how their minds worked. His short stories are well-finished and are integrated works of art. Most of his stories depend upon characters i.e. they are the short stories of characters.

Bond was born on May 19, 1934 at Kasauli, Himachal Pradesh. He is the eldest son of late Aubrey Alexander Bond, a British officer in Royal Air Force in India. His sister Ellen was a little handicapped child with defective vision and initial signs of epilepsy. Ellen lived with Granny (Grandmother) and brother William at Calcutta, but Bond grew-up in Jamnagar (Gujarat), Dehradun and Shimla.

Bond got the Sahitya Akademy Award (1992) for the book Our Trees Still Grow in Dehra. Two of his novels The Room on The Roof and Vagrants I the Valley were published in one volume in 1993. The novella A Handful of Nuts was written 1995 over a period of three months and half, when icy winds and snowstorms kept him confined to his small cottage in the hills.

Honoured with the prestigious Padamshree in 1999 for his lifetime contribution to Indian English Literature, he has cast an indelible imprint on the contemporary literary scene. On the occasion of his sixty-seventh birthday, May 19, 2001, he gifted two of his books Friends in Small Places and When Darkness Falls to his avid readers. Just when one may think that the veteran writer has run out of stock, he is back with great intensity and freshness of narration.

The story "The Thief" reveals same predicament of human psychology. The story moves about the conflict of a thief whose habitual urge to steal forces him to rob his very friend, Arun. But his simple logic, "I am getting out of practice...He does not even pay me," (Bond : 1988 : 40) evades when he feels guilty of robbing the very embodiment of trust in life. He wails:

> He was the most trusting person I had ever met...
> It is easy to rob a greedy man...but it is difficult to
> rob a poor person, even one who really doesn't care
> if he is robbed. (Bond : 1988 : 40)

The story aims to reveal that even a thief can discriminate panic reaction of the face of a person robbed from the shocking indifference or lack of reaction of his friend towards the abominable act. The thief fails to enjoy his accomplishment because the target is not a sufferer at all. The story presents a drama of complex human psyche. The moment thief realizes that it is he who had been robbed of trust, the most valuable thing in life, he repents and returns to regain it. The story indicates that the line that divides a man as good or bad is very thin almost indiscernible and one can dodge it easily.

Glossary

Grunting : to produce a low rough noise
Incentive : which encourages a person to do something
Flicked : to move or hitch with a short sudden movement
Conspicuous : quite noticeable and tending to attract attention
Vagrant : a person who is homeless as well as poor

(XI)
The Voice of God

(Khushwant Singh)

Khushwant Singh, the son of Sir Shobha Singh a prominent builder in Lutyens' Delhi, was born on 2nd February in Hadali, Punjab (Pakistan). He is a well-known Indian novelist and journalist in English. He was educated at Government College, Lahore and St. Stephen's College before reading for the Bar at King's College, Cambridge. He served as editor of several well-known literary and news magazines, including the government journal 'The Illustrated Weekly of India'. His weekly column 'With malice towards one and all' carried by several newspapers, is among the most widely-read columns in the country. He was awarded the Padma Bhushan in 1974 and an even more prestigious honour, the Padma Vibhushan. He is best known for his trenchant secularism, humour and abiding love of poetry. His works include, 'Train to Pakistan', 'I Shall not hear the Nightingale', 'The Voice of God and other Short Stories' and outstanding translations of Sikh religious texts and Urdu poetry.

During the Raj the twin villages in Punjab generally referred to as just Bhamba are rudely awakened from their somnambulist lifestyle and plunged into a flurry of political activity with the arrival of a succession of political groups that come to canvass for their respective candidates in the forthcoming elections to the Punjab Legislative Assembly.

The first group represents the face of colonial power and brute force in the person of Mr. Forsythe, the English Deputy Commissioner accompanied by Sardar Ganda Singh, the most hated patron of thugs in the district. The latter, an Honorary Magistrate and a big landowner who lived in and owned the neighbouring village and liquor shops, had been nominated by the leaders of the Sikh community with the full approval of the Government. Next day a second group of young men in Gandhi caps dressed in khadi clothes representing the Nationalist party arrive with their nominee Sardar Kartar Singh, Advocate supported by Seth Sukhtankar, a well-known Nationalist leader and also a millionaire industrialist. Each group slanders against each other but both the candidates agree to keep the third group-the Kisan-out. Finally, one spring afternoon Baba Ram Singh, the Kisan, who had courted arrest several times during peasant movements and now homeless, arrives alone at Bhamba to ask the villagers for their votes. He was revered and popularly known as Babaji because of his age and piety. He promises to fight for their liberation from foreigners as well as exploiting landlords.Unlike the other political contestants he never even mentions the names of his rival candidates.

At the conclusion, in choosing the Kisan, the voice of the people -the voice of God is cruelly silenced by the might of both colonialism and capitalism when the rigged results announce the victory of Sardar Ganda Singh and the forfeit of Baba Ram Singh's deposit. The force of the irony with its implied anguish at the end of the tale is reinforced through the subtlety and poignancy of its narrative technique.

The narrative illustrates how the ancient forces of greed and violence in humans feed into colonialism and even the national bourgeoisie who claim to be passionately anti-British emerge as another face of imperial hegemony.

Glossary

Brawl : to fight

Siesta : mid day or afternoon not

Canvassed : to ask for vote

Ploud : soothing, calmness
Imminent : event that is going to take place
Seditions : an act of treason or betrayal

(XII)
SEXY
(Jhumpa Lahiri)

Jhumpa Lahiri, the daughter of Indian Bengali immigrants to America, was born as Nilanjana Sudeshna in London, England in 1967. Her parents moved to the United States when she was three. Her kindergarten teacher in Kingston decided to call her by her pet name Jhumpa as it was easier to pronounce than her official name. Her debut short story collection, Interpreter of Maladies (1999) won the 2000 Pulitzer Prize for Fiction, and her first novel, The Namesake (2003), was adapted into the popular film of the same name.

The two short stories Interpreter of Maladies and Sexy taken from her debut short story collection, address sensitive diasporic 'maladies' in the lives of Indian immigrants. Each is both an individual story and, explicitly, a cultural narrative. Lahiri's works confirm a hybridity between diasporic and domiciled consciousness as seen in the works of various other diasporian authors like Amitava Ghosh, Salman Rushdie, Tabish Khair, Aga Shahid Ali, Sonali Bose who are national, not nationalistic, inclusive not parochial, respecting the local while being ecumenical, celebrating human values and Indian pluralism. The third space thus created becomes permanent which non-Diasporas fail to fill. This hybridity is subversive as it resists and interrogates authoritarianism and challenges official truths.

Lahiri's works mostly revolve around Indian emigrant parents to America and their struggle not only to raise a family in a country very different from theirs but also to keep their children acquainted with the Indian culture and traditions. Her characters, often Indian immigrants to America, strive to navigate between the cultural values of their birthplace and their adopted home. The first generation of Indian immigrants struggle to keep their children close to them even after they have grown up in order to hang on to the Indian tradition of a joint family, where the parents, their children and the children's family live under the same roof. They are forced to face the dilemmas and the inevitability of the disconnection between first and second generation immigrants in the process of occupying and negotiating between the cultural spaces of the two worlds.

Like Interpreter of Maladies and other diasporic literature, Lahiri's short story Sexy is less concerned with a problematic hero/

heroine than a problematic collective situation. Even though it is a story of an individual and that too a white American woman, the diasporic sensibility is ever present in the constant elision of the narrative between the individual and the communal, the personal and the collective. The author may be seen as one who stands in for a whole community of which she is a part.

Sexy deals with inter-racial sexuality of the Indian males' desire for white women, seen simultaneously from the two polarities of both the American and Indian cultures. The story set in Boston is ostensibly about the individual experience of a young single American woman's affair with a married Indian Bengali but the narrative navigates between the cultural values of the strict traditions inherited by the Indians in exile and the baffling alien cultural context of the New World. The narrative weaves through the two world views represented by Laxmi and her office friend Miranda and presents two almost identical experiences of Indian male marital infidelity. One experience is presented in the indirect form of Laxmi's loquacious judgmental narrative of her cousin's husband's infidelity while the other experience, is a more empathetic account of Miranda's growing relationship with Dev. The indirect form of the narrative (running parallel to the main one) serves to help the reader see the problem as a communal one where the peripheral culture under threat tends to vilify the culture at the centre even as it tries to mimic it. This schizophrenic state or the double consciousness or the split consciousness of being Indian and American is the result of the diasporic individual's desire to combine two cultures and languages without abandoning either. The main narrative on the other hand, serves to individualise the problem by not seeing the white woman as evil / temptress simply because she belongs to an alien culture. Laxmi's ignorance of Miranda's affair with a married Indian male accentuates not only the contrast but the irony of the two narratives. In spite of being fully aware of the pleasure principle of their relationship and a total lack of commitment in Dev's attitude, Miranda allows her interest in her lover to deepen. The introduction of Rohin, the cousin's seven year old son, into the main narrative brings about an elision between the communal and the individual but from opposite perspectives. His naive half-understood use of the word 'sexy' to describe Miranda as she baby-sits for his mother serves as an ironic echo of Dev's use of the same word during the lovers' visit to the Mapparium. Finding themselves alone after the departure of the other tourists, standing thirty feet apart on the 'acoustic' bridge, Dev seductively whispers to Miranda, the words, 'You're sexy'. In contrast, the childish explanation of the word 'sexy' by the seven year-old shocks Miranda into realizing the meaninglessness and futility of such a relationship, a dilemma which cuts across cultural barriers.

Glossary

Soliciting : urging

Pledges : something given as security

Tote bag : carry-bag

Pantyhose : one piece garment consisting of underpants and stretchable stockings the T underground train, commuter rail

Carousel : a rotating conveyor

Paranoid : mentally disturbed

Pulled pork : preparation of pork, usually the shoulder, cooked on low heat over a long period of time, enabling the meat to become tender enough to be 'pulled' or broken into individual pieces.

Sangria : a West-Indian drink of wine, diluted, sweetened and spiced

MFA : Museum of Fine Arts

Mapparium : a three-storey tall glass globe of stained glass that is viewed from a 30 feet long bridge through its interior. It is a unique and famous exhibit at the Christian Science Centre in Boston, Massachusetts. Built in 1935, it shows the political world as it was at that time.

Sheer : thin, fine material

Cocktail dress : woman's short evening dress for an early-evening cocktail party

Foie gras : (fwa gra-part of the full French phrase - pate de foie gras) goose liver paste filling the Charles: the name of a river

Deli : a store which sells delicacies of fine food

Baguette : a variety of loaf bread with a crispy crust

Tortes : cake made with many eggs and ground nuts

Pesto : a sauce or paste of crushed herbs and garlic

Mascarpone : triple cream cheese

Development : (American) real estate area - a colony or block

Siding : a covering of sheet materials to prevent rain or wind infiltration in a house

Dowel : a headless pin of wood or metal for fastening things together by fitting into a hole in each

Filofax : a trademark for a compact loose-leaf binder

	containing sheets of paper in different colours, used as a personal portable filing system and address book
Sitcom	: (informal) situation comedy on television
Harem pants	: the Indian 'shalwar'
Pita bread	: the Indian 'phulka' or 'chapati'
Woodwork	: wood hoardings
Layover	: a brief stop during a journey
Herringbone	: a pattern of rows of short slanted parallel lines
Double-parked	: parked alongside another parked vehicle
Almanac	: an annual publication including calendar with weather forecasts astronomical events and other related tabular informations
Rice cakes	: the Indian 'idli'
Sweatpants	: cotton pants worn specially as casual wear or for sport
Comforter	: polyester filled quilt

(XIII)
'Interpreter of Maladies'

(Jhumpa Lahiri)

The narrative of this short story seen through Mr. Kapasi's perspective explores the difference between the two cultures of the homeland and that of the adopted country through the domiciled consciousness of Mr. and Mrs. Das, a very young American couple of Indian origin ('perhaps not even thirty') born and brought up in the United States. Together with their two sons and a daughter, they come to India as American tourists. Mr. Kapasi, their tour guide, drives them in his bulky white Ambassador to the Sun temple at Konarak in the mid-July heat. The Das family shows no attempt, conscious or otherwise, to assert ethnic identity in terms of the 'homeland' and neither do they suffer from a sense of cultural dislocation as the second generation has less of adaptation problems having been born and raised in America. But their parents after retirement have returned to their 'home' country to live in 'Assansol' and visited by their children every two years. Even though the Das family may look Indian the cultural assimilation in Mr. Das and his children appears complete. Their code of behaviour and mode of dress is typically American as is their speech. It is in the character of Mrs. Das, seemingly indifferent to everything around her, that the ambivalence over identity emerges quite suddenly in her unexpected revelation to Mr. Kapasi of the eight year old baggage of painful experience she carried of her secret past of one night stand of which Bobby, her second son, was the result.

Mr. Kapasi who in his youth had dreamed of being an interpreter for diplomats and dignitaries ended up with an 'alternative career' working for a non-Gujarati-speaking doctor as the interpreter of the Gujarati patients' maladies which Mrs. Das finds to be 'romantic'. She senses the gravity of such a responsibility which demands accuracy of interpretation as an effective means of communication. Swamped by the anxiety of cultural dislocation, without anyone to turn to, she turns expectantly to Mr. Kapasi, a virtual stranger, to structure her feelings by interpreting her personal 'malady' and offering her some kind of remedy to assuage her deep anxiety and psychic insecurity. In spite of being almost old enough to be her father Mr. Kapasi finds himself drawn to Mrs. Das. But he, however, is firmly rooted in a firm, well-defined convention-bound complex societal structure that gives him the psychological comfort that Mrs. Das is sorely in need of. When he questions her whether it is 'guilt' rather than 'pain' that she feels, the inadequacy of his conventional structuring of feelings results in her cold silence and immediate withdrawal of interest in him as an interpreter of maladies. This signifies not Mr. Kapasi's failure but the failure of the system to which he belongs, to accommodate the ever-shifting system of blurred values and boundaries of the diasporic sensibility.

Glossary

Translucent : imperfectly transparent

Visor : the peak of a cap used as a shade against the sun

Flexed : tilted

Butterscotch : a kind of toffee containing much butter

Undershirt : a man's collarless undergarment which may or may not have sleeves

Calico : plain white cotton cloth

Chafe : to heat of wear by rubbing

Cranklike : like an arm on a handle

Pinafore : a skirt hung from the shoulders

Emaciated : extremely thin

Assiduously : tirelessly

Etymology : the science or investigation of the origin or root of a word

Grammar school : a higher school in which academic subjects predominate

Fritters : a piece of fruit fried in batter (paste)

Gotten	: American usage of 'got'
Flank	: to be on the side of
Medallion	: a round ornament or design of a similar form
Friezes	: any band of painted or sculptured decoration
Niche	: (pron: neesh or nich) a recess in the wall
Amulet	: a charm carried about a person
Plummeted	: plunged head-long
Hewn	: cut, shaped
Defile	: a long narrow pass or way with a narrow front
Harried	: harassed
Plaid skirt	: a checked skirt
Arcade	: a row of arches on columns
Welts	: lashes, blows
Stomping	: stamping

□